Emily

Emily

Arnold G. Ramos

Dedication

I hope my mother was still alive. She would be happy with what I have achieved in writing prose books. Because she was my first fan when I was just starting out. And for the first time, she was with me when I was paid for my writing to appear in the comics in Life love Comics. Because of that, my mother gave me a second-hand typewriter. That made me happy, even though she is in the afterlife, this is my dream for her.

Contents

Table of Contents

difficult to wake in the morning. Michael had become a headache to Laura.

7. In Germany, even when he was at work, his mind was far away from what he was thinking, aside from his son. He couldn't take away from his mind the whole of Emily's face. A smile on his cheek drew the pleasure that was making him happy.

8. In the courtroom, everyone was holding back their breaths. Even Luigi didn't know what to do. He could do nothing but sympathize with Emily's condition when he saw her entered the courtroom handcuffed. But Luigi tried to be calm in court.

9. At eight o'clock in the morning, Alexandra angrily went to the door to see who had come. "Good morning! Emily, is she there?"

10. Luigi quickly followed his instructions on how to plant rice until he realizes that he was capable and fast in planting, something he secretly enjoyed.

11. In frustration, Emily's smile widened, and Rosanna noticed it. It was enough for her to know where she was in Luigi's heart.

12. .Emily got busy caring for Michael. After leaving school, they hurried down so Michael can play in the park.

13. Emily nearly pulled out a thorn in the chest when it was getting dark. That's all she had to wait for her to get out of Laura's house right away. Her speed was just as fast as the lightning so she could go farild's usual way when with Emily. While there was a chance.

14. When Emily's leg was finally healed, she began to bring the child again to Laura's house. She also had difficulty in dealing with Mauro. Once again, she became annoyed again to Laura's lover. But in those moments, she decided not to be complacent with him.

15. In Luigi and Michael's mansion, they returned since Laura's death. They stayed at the palace even though it was too big for only two people and housekeepers.

Summary

Emily, in her adolescence, had to help her parents. They were rich in earthly livelihood. But they could not sell their vast land to start their lives. That's what his father, Delfin, told him not to interfere with what their mother inherited. So, Emily decided to travel to Italy. Incidentally, her aunt was there for a long time. So, when she had a direct-hire, her aunt quickly helped her. Her aunt was serving the friend of Luigi for a long time. Luigi got married to Laura, who was a famous model and Italian actress.

But coincidentally, Luigi suddenly fell in love with Emily despite having a son, Michael, something Laura didn't like. For Laura, it was a great insult that Emily replaced her, who was a BABYSITTER.

Prologue

Emily did not expect that Michael, the boy who always accompanied her, would avoid her. She was just surprised because of the loss of her mother, Laura. The boy thought that Michael was the one who killed his mother. So he avoided her. Emily was very hurt because she loved him. Even though she was not his real mother. In the end, he chased her and they went to the Philippines to find Emily. But unfortunately, Emily's father, Delfin, was angry because he was imprisoned in Italy for kidnapping. It was a matter of Delfin not accepting Emily's father at that time, he drove away Emily's guest, Luigi. Instead, he axed him on the side of the bamboo pillar placed there

Chapter One

Inside the house of an Italian family, there is Emily, who works as a nanny or 'Yaya,' a similar term known in her native place far away from Pampanga.

Here enters a simple town girl who made to fly to Italy full of fear and anxiety.

It is her first time to take care of a child who is not her child or of her relative. What only in her mind is that she can take care of a child since she took care of her youngest sibling. She also knows how to stop a crying baby.

At the age of twenty-two, Emily is just starting to act like a fine lady. She knows nothing about love, nor she never been experienced to admire some boys in their place, which made people mistaken her to be arrogant and snobbish. She is also inside the house all the time.

Not knowing her age, she was used to doing chores, so she is no longer a problem of her mother.

Her mother taught her to do housework because it was the order of her siblings and cousins who had come first to Italy. She must be skilled in that so that she can work in the said country and her employer will like her.

Emily's family is not that wealthy. So, she bravely presented herself to her cousin to help her get to Europe.

Her cousin said that at the time of needing help from her boss's relatives, she would call immediately. So, she never wondered if her cousin would tell her she was coming to Italy.

By the time her visa to Italy was issued, she was full of excitement. She did not expect her papers to come out, saying that she could work abroad. So, she prayed that she would get on the plane that she had just gazed at in the air passing over the roof of their house.

She thinks it's all a dream when she gazes into the air that you can see only a pigeon flying under the clouds. So, to make sure she didn't just dream, she even pinched herself.

She was nervous as soon as she was already outside the airport in Rome. Relatives of her aunt, who were her father's sister, escorted her to the airport.

She couldn't even recognize her aunt because of how long they hadn't met. Her aunt didn't also get a chance to have a vacation in Pampanga.

She was not surprised when her aunt and cousin Alexandra approached her. Onboard, a 'Fiat' model car took them to their Trastevere apartment.

Here, Emily stayed less than two days before she enters for work. Her workplace is also near Trastevere.

Emily almost wanted to lose her consciousness when she saw the seeming palace home she will use to live as a babysitter. She felt like the house is a prince's home, which she had never seen such a large house aside from movies.

Even in her dream, she never expected that she would come here. She also held her aunt's arms firmly seemingly she didn't want to go on. But she wanted to change her family's life in Pampanga. That is why she came to fulfill her promise to her parents in helping in paying for the education of her younger siblings.

Their new boss welcomed them as architect Luigi and Laura, a famous model and artist. Emily didn't expect that a famous actress like Laura Papi would be able to get close enough. She already once watched Laura join a global beauty contest that she had to come down first for others to see her.

But what gave her more attention was her rounded stomach that at any time it could come out. Her employers had already given up the housework. One of the housemates in the mansion, Doray, immediately showed her around. Emily was almost astonished at the size of her room. She didn't expect this to be her bedroom. Unlike in the Philippines, they are almost overcrowded. But she ignored everything. What was more important for her is to send her first paycheck so that her siblings, whom she had left in the Philippines, could start school. Incidentally, that was the first day of her work. Emily secretly smiled at her sudden obligation to her family.

At first, Emily couldn't sleep since that was her first day at her boss's house. The sadness in her round face made her feel more alone. Especially, she is longing for her parents and siblings. She couldn't stop herself from crying.

She assured herself that she would soon be used to live the kind of life there. She had to be brave for the long days she would spend in Italy. It was almost a month later when Emily became accustomed to life in Rome. She is already looking for her sweet-smelling room, which relieves her fatigue.

After all, her lady boss has not yet given birth. It's almost early next month, but she feels like she's working on a construction site in her intense work such as cleaning around their yard and planting at the small part of their backyard.

But she did not care of all those sufferings, even though three of her workmates in the mansion were on sudden vacation. What matters to her is that her bosses like her and she must show that she doesn't need to be instructed from time to time.

Time passed, and she was able to get all the work done. Even the markets frequented by Filipinos, even the gambling place and to pass through Your Fermi. She was thinking about the self-discipline she had never forgotten to bring to Europe. It was late at night when Emily returned to her boss's house. With her work breaks every Thursday and Sunday, she used to go out frequently with her cousins and aunt.

Wherever there were a banquet and baptism, she was always with her cousins and aunts. She was with them anywhere as long as they are still together as family relatives. Everywhere she went, men could not ignore her. Paolo was one of those who accidentally glanced at Emily. He quickly winked to her, but Emily didn't show any smile to the man, she doesn't know or see all her life. Emily immediately turned to her aunt and turned her attention to others. She never attempted to look back to the man who wanted to capture her heart.

She showed a fierce face showing that she cannot be caught by any in just a wink when the man winked again to her.

Emily quickly got up from her seat with her aunt next to her. She approached the man who winked at her.

"Pak!" "Is that what you are looking for?!"

"Huh?!"

Paolo quickly stood up and left the crowd. Even though he was surprised, he did nothing with Emily's quick slap. Everyone was shocked at what they didn't expect to happen in those moments.

"What is it? Why did you slap that young man away?" asked Emily's aunt Ana.

"He winks at me. Maybe, he thought he could get me in his winks! So, I approached him and slapped him to answer his winks!"

"Oh, my dear!" said her aunt angrily. "You're embarrassing! You know we're just new here. You mistreated their guest!"

"Hmmph! Don't care about them. So, the next time he sees me, he will avoid me."

"If by chance, he will do it again, he could not just only take a slap from me!' Emily couldn't help but chuckle.

"You are too fearless. Can you reduce your fierce? Beware, you might find your counterpart!" scoffed by aunt Ana.

Emily ignored everything, even the threat of her aunt. Until they are walking down the street, his aunt had not finished yelling on her. Emily just pretended of not hearing anything.

In her room, Emily couldn't sleep. She suddenly felt pity for the man she had slapped. She regretted why she did that. But sometimes, her mind denies it.

"Hmmph! It was good for him, so he would never repeat it to me. He'll be reminded when he sees me again!

Whatever she does, she did not feel sleepy for some unknown reason.

"Sorry, whoever you are, I was just shocked. Promise, I will never do it again. I'm sorry!"

That's all what she repeatedly says to herself, It was almost dawn when she felt sleepy. It was only then when Emily slept. Though she slept late, she still used to wake up early. She prepared the table and made warm milk for herself. It's almost lunchtime when her boss gets up. Being an architect, he is just at home doing his drawings of house plans.

His wife, on the other hand, was on leave because she was pregnant.

She is just waiting for her delivery and will once again enter into a modelling and acting career.

So, Emily is confident that she has no problem in seeing much of her work in the house but to think more of herself. She used to clean quickly the living room filled with clutter and toys left behind by the couple's nephews.

Emily didn't even feel annoyed even though she didn't know where to put things that weren't in the closet. She placed some toys of her master's nephews to the nursery room. Even though the baby is not yet born, the room was already full of baby kinds of stuff and toys. Obviously, the couple is preparing the bedroom of their child ahead of time.

Emily didn't notice that her smile was different every time she enters the nursery room. She was excited about the arrival of the new prince inside that home. Being fond of her nephews and nieces, she knew for herself that she could take good care of the baby.

One day, Laura did not expect that she is already going to give birth. Unfortunately, both of their drivers were on leave that day, and Luigi was out of town for his work commitment.

"Emily, please call a taxi. It's time for my delivery!" ordered by Donya Laura.

"Yes, ma'am! Right away!"

Even though Emily was in disarray, she still knows what to do. She also managed to call a taxi for her boss. Laura answered the phone when it rang. Emily couldn't yet be able to answer the operator's questions, so she quickly handed the phone to Laura. Once settled, the taxi arrived shortly.

Emily backed up her lady boss who was in so much pain until she got into the car.

Emily was terrified. She thought of the situation of giving birth suffering from too much pain.

But the desire to see the new prince she would take care of overshadowed her. Everyone was no longer allowed to come along when Laura entered the delivery room. Even her relatives are no longer allowed to enter. So, they just waited in the hallway of the hospital.

Emily quickly returned to a large bag containing the personal belongings of the new prince of the palace. The couple will have a male offspring because that's what they were expecting as to what the result of Laura's ultrasound had shown. So, they were delighted that Laura and Luigi would have a baby boy.

From Germany, Luigi quickly returned to Italy even before his work ended there. He longs to see his child.

Inside the baby room, Luigi always waves at his son inside the incubator. Sometimes, the baby smiles at him, which made him happy even though he knew that the baby could not yet recognize him.

Luigi took the child out of the hospital. His longing led him until to the nursery room before he returns to Germany.

It was enough for him to return to his unfinished commitment to Germany. He just thought that he would be back to Italy as soon as his work was over.

Emily was the companion of the baby in the nursery room. Laura wanted it that way. She wants Emily to be like the child's mother first when she returns to modelling. Thus, Emily's joy cannot be painted as she cares for her boss' son.

She would often sleep with the child in her bed by the time Laura and Luigi left. Suddenly, she thought of her nephew that she too often slept with when his parents are away. So, she already gets used to the kids.

It looks like Emily is the mother of the child. She is the one who changes diapers when the baby is soiled, bottle-feeds, and she also brings the baby herself to the hospital when he is sick. She even personally took care of the schedule of the vaccine shots of the baby.

She almost knows what the child needs in the day to day doing it. Because of this, Emily is secretly pleased.

One day, she didn't realize that the child was almost on the edge of the crib. The baby is trying to stand by himself. Emily enjoyed it a lot. Whenever she sees that the child is slowly moving closer to her, she gives him always a warm kiss.

Instead of taking advantage of the opportunity for the baby to sleep, she spends most of the time cleaning the house.

Emily spends a lot of time cleaning the bathroom. She doesn't want to see even a single strand of hair. When she was sure it was all clean, she quickly left the bathroom and headed to the kitchen to prepare lunch for the couple.

The couple often eats blanched vegetables. Hence, Emily had little meal preparation. The couple's second plate is fried beef steak. After the couple had eaten their meals, their boss Luigi used to have his coffee. So, Emily already knew what she was going to do by the time her boss finished eating.

Although she is tired, she made sure she served the couple well. After lunchtime, it was time for her break. In her room, her boss Luigi accidentally passed by the hallway. He carefully closed the door of Emily's room.

In those moments, Emily was in wonder.

"Who opened the door?" she asked herself.

She got up and made sure the door was locked and quickly returned to the bed and laid down with the baby.

Chapter Two

In the kid's room, Emily barely leaves the baby next to her because she is so happy about it. She always touches the baby's pointed nose and even his red lips that look like apples. She also stares at his rounded face. The child is close to her, even though her stay is not yet that long. She wants to embrace and kiss him, but she won't do it because it's the baby's bedtime. Even though she knew she had something to do outside the room, she is there for hours. She has the clothes to be ironed and started to fold them. She prefers to fold first the clothes of the baby because she enjoys looking at it.

She then followed in folding her employers' clothes but stopped when she noticed that it was getting dark. Gradually, she put away the things until she went into the kitchen to prepare meals for the three of them. She only stopped when she heard the child cries, so she hurried to the baby's room.

Emily went back into the kitchen when she saw that the baby was asleep again. The 'lady tata' was secretly delighted with the 'cute' baby she was taking care.

Emily was busy preparing dinner and was surprised when Señora Laura suddenly arrived.

"What are you doing?" Señora Laura asked.

"I am preparing food for your dinner," Emily replied.

"Va bene forse, il bambino dove si trova. Come sta?"

"Ancora nella sua stanza. Voglio che tu prendi!"

"No, appena preparato il caffè!"

"Ci, señora!"

Emily quickly agreed to make coffee. Señora Laura sat in the chair next to Emily to wait for her coffee. Not long after, after drinking the coffee, her señora quickly returned to her room.

She didn't even spend time to see her son, though she could pass the child's room. Emily noticed it. But Emily thought she might not want to disturb the baby's sleep. Emily quickly returned to the kitchen to cook. She cooked first the vegetables that the architect loves to eat. Then, followed the meat placed on the paddle and put on fire for a long time on the open burner. It also took a few moments before she prepared the dinner table, and the man whom Laura waited for, just arrived. The couple liked the pasta that Emily prepared for them. The peeled garlic was sautéed with olive oil until golden brown before putting away from fire. Then she added the olive oil to the cooked pasta. Soon, the meat extracted hot from the paddle was also ready.

Everything that Emily prepared was like a hurricane that just passed by. Emily secretly enjoyed her prepared meals for the couple. After they asked for hot tea, she prepared a meal for herself. But before she could do that, she temporarily took a peek at the baby and assured that he was deeply asleep. Emily quickly headed to the kitchen and ate. She then inserted the dirty dishes and utensils into the machine right away.

Emily quickly returned to the room to sleep with the baby. She laughed secretly at herself. She thought she is better than the birth mother of the child. It looked like the baby wanted her tata to breastfeed him every time he cries in the middle of the night.

She immediately stands up when the baby yells to have his wet diaper change. In this day-to-day routine, she already knows every detail of taking care of the child. She thought of her brother on how she had taken care of him. Her mother took care of them at night after her work in their place in Pampanga as an ordinary clerk in the municipality. Emily just sighed when she noticed that she was the one now taking care at night.

So, what Emily does is to give the child a sudden hug and kiss, and the child likes it, too. In his first words, Emily laughed because he calls Emily 'tata.' She did not realize that the child grew up so fast and his child approach to her is still the same.

What Emily can only give to the child is the genuine love and care for the child. The child is always neat and clean even when he is playing for hours and spreading his toys around the house. And it's okay for Emily even the house is messy because it makes the kid happy and this is all she can give. Señora Laura sometimes stumbled over her child's toys. As a result, her head grew hot, and her son Michael quickly went to his room. When she opened the door, she did not immediately see the child, but his tata was folding the clothes.

"Dove i più giovani, Señora Laura?"

"Lui non è qui, che fuori?"

"Insegnare che si cura, poi si sdraiò a giocare i suoi

giocattoli, oppure si può."

"Organizzare per lui!"

"Ci señora!"

Signed quickly out of the child's room, she continued to leave the house. By that time, the car was ready for her to use. As a model, Laura has to be beautiful in front of people, especially her fans. She must always be pretty in the eyes of others. That is why, in her surprise, her worries wept away at how quickly her former body was back in a short time. They did not expect Laura to be pregnant. But the time came when she had to take a break from modelling and give herself time to give birth. She had to go back to her old beautiful self because her popularity as a model was more important to her.

Laura was thirsty for the praise and applause of the people. Because she's just a daughter of a low-income family so it's not easy to give up on the world she lives in today.

Laura is afraid to be infamous. That is why she always accept invitations from different occasions for her popularity. She promised herself that her family would never return to their old, hard, and bad lives.

Her only investment to get to the top is her beautiful face. To her, everyone worshipped and admired her. Thus, Luigi, one of the most famous and best architects in their area, fell in love with her.

Luigi has made many private and government properties. People always talk about the projects he does. They still remember the greatness of his profession every time they saw tall buildings, whether public or private, in their place.

Luigi's popularity and passion made him possess one of the most beautiful faces in their area. That was Laura. But after Laura gave birth, they seldom meet due to the large size of their mansion. So, it is not surprising that they cannot pay attention to the child and cannot see him growing up.

Emily's three workmates arrived at the mansion from vacation in the Philippines. So, she will now spend all of her time taking care of Michael.

"You are lucky, and you will only take care of the child. While we will clean the whole mansion." the old maid Minerva told Emily.

"Did you know that when you were not all here, I was the only one who did all that. I have no companions here! I have no complaints either about my tasks such as cooking, babysitting, and cleaning the whole house. Wouldn't it be great if I gave you back your throne then?" Emily fiercely said to Minerva. "It took you all so long in the Philippines, almost a year!"

"Hasn't Señora got you a companion? Maybe she's saving! Minerva once said then turned away.

Emily turned away also. She didn't spend much time arguing with Minerva anymore.

In those moments, the height of his pout nearly reached the sky. Minerva didn't even show it to Emily. But she soon approached to Emily too.

"Sorry, I didn't mean what I said earlier," Minerva humbly said.

"It's okay, and it's nothing."

"When's your day-off? Do you want to go with me? I'll introduce you to my Italian boyfriend!" Minerva proudly said to Emily.

"Oh my! You go alone, I have no interest to that. Maybe your boyfriend will like me!" Emily and Minerva laughed.

"Uhm, I'll give it to you then!"

The two laughed together.

Emily and Minerva noticed both that they were feeling better, and Emily knew it all.

Emily wants to feel at ease with her co-workers. Although her co-workers were serving in the mansion for the longest time, Minerva immediately asked for apologies because of her conduct. Minerva wants them to be patient with her because her behaviour is just like that. On Thursday afternoon, they went out together. They did not go to Minerva's boyfriend but to Sta. Prudenziana in Via Urbana. Here they devoted their time to give service to God.

It was dark at night when they returned to the mansion. Their faces, especially Emily, were filled with joy as they were able to serve the Lord.

She hadn't been to church for a long time. She couldn't get out, especially when she was alone in the mansion.

So, she pushed to her limit in serving the church during the day she had her off.

But she could not take away the child she was taking care of from her mind. She was sure that the child would have tantrums. He couldn't eat without Emily on her side. Even his mother and father were shocked at the child's behaviour. He could only be stopped when her tata, Emily, is there.

"Eat now. I've prepared your meal." Emily said sweetly to Michael. The child acted and stood up quickly. For that boy, Emily's words were laws he was waiting for — a doctrine full of love.

Emily knew immediately what the child likes. He knew how to melt the kid's heart. Laura and Luigi were always surprised that Emily seemed to have a strange 'magic' on how she disciplines Michael.

What the child always does was to litter and play all day in their mansion. Yet, they were happy during those times and the child used to eat even without them. But it was hard on parents like Laura that her child was unfriendly to her. The boy was closer to his tata than to her.

One day Emily noticed that Laura had a mean look on her. In the corner of her eye, she could see it, but she just ignored it. Señora Laura looked at her differently. There was a little bit of bitterness in his heart, but she just gave it all to God. She just put in her mind that it was not her fault that the boy was closer to her. Minerva had all noticed Señora Laura's strange gaze toward Emily.

"It looks like our lady boss' blood is boiling because of you," Minerva said.

"Why? I didn't do anything to her, huh! There is no reason for her to be angry at me," defended Emily. Minerva walked away when she noticed that Señora Laura as coming back in the kitchen. She even didn't bid goodbye to Emily.

"Si può prendere la mia sigaretta alla mia macchina!" commanded señora to Emily.

"Ci Senora!"

Chapter Three

Emily quickly obeyed the command of Señora Laura. A few moments later, she returned carrying a cigarette she took inside the car. Emily noticed that her lady boss looked strange to her. But, she didn't let Laura know that she was looking at her. Her boss left without even thanking her. Emily just shrugged to what her boss said. She had just thought that her boss wouldn't do it if she is not the nanny of the, so Emily expected it. What matters most to her is that Michael was giving her care and respect. She seemed to be his parent. And so, she was enjoying the great love of the child she was taking care of.

Here, she secretly smiled and felt tireless when the child is showing affection to Emily, even in front of Laura. This was probably why the mother is jealous of her.

It didn't strike her mind that her boss would think that they were going be rival to Michael. What matters to her was that the child loves her and respects her. For him, that was enough. Many days and years passed. They noticed that the two couples were always arguing, a thing that the child was not accustomed to. After a while, the servants in the mansion were ignoring them. They were now accustomed to their quarrel.

"When are you going to stop in modeling? You are talking to any man!" Jealousy popped into Luigi's mouth.

"You know, that's part of my life. It will never be taken away from me!" defended Laura.

"And if you are not drunk, you come home early at dawn! You even beat me!"

"I'm tired. Let's talk tomorrow. I don't have time to listen to you now!" Laura told her husband. As Laura entered the room, she hurried to one of its doors. She changed her clothes into nighties from long-cluttered cabinets there.

She faced the mirror while removing the red kinds of stuff from her round face. Soon, she went out of the comfort room wearing the thinnest cloth covering her body.

The radiance of her body that everyone is crazy about is still visible. When Luigi saw it, he turned away and covered his face with a pillow so he could not see his wife's warm body.

It was Luigi who turned off the light near Laura's head, and she didn't like it. Laura climbed into the bed. Even though Laura made the bed sound squeaky, Luigi just ignored, and he even got farther away to Laura.

Laura's charm was tempting. Laura moved closer to her husband and placed her muzzle on Luigi's ear. But something different happened. Luigi quickly stood up.

"I'm tired. I'll sleep in the other room."

"I'm your wife!"

"Is there a spouse who goes home earlier than her husband? Then you wonder why the kid feels so far away from you? Both of you don't even meet! What do you think is the time now?"

"You are saying a lot! If you want, you sleep outside!"

Luigi didn't talk anymore. He noticed that Laura was drunk. He knew that it would be hard to argue with Laura, who was drunk and almost not in herself.

So, he just decided to get out of their room and to spend the night in the guest room. This made Laura even more annoyed. As Luigi closed the door, Laura threw the pillow to it.

The next day, at the front of the dining table, the Luigi and Laura were silent. Luigi got his coffee first. He just continued sipping his coffee while staring at the newspaper he was reading. Although he knew that Laura had arrived, he did not pay his respects to his wife. Laura looked differently. She knew it was her fault and had no right to feel dominant over her husband. So, Laura was the first to break the silence.

"I have a plan to go to my mom because it's her birthday. Would you like to join us? I plan to have Michael and his tata go with me."

"You all go. I have something to take care of." Luigi said.

"They might look for you. You know, you're the first one my family is looking for if they don't see you with me.'

"Just make a way," Luigi said and turned away as his coffee ran out.

At that moment, Laura was surprised at what Luigi told her. But Laura remained calm. She did not address her husband's anger. Shortly after that, she headed to her child's room to accompany her to her mother, waiting for their arrival. In those moments, the child was still asleep even though they knew the sun was high. Laura looked at Emily.

"You, too, get dressed! You'll come with us to the house of Michael's grandmother," Laura told Emily.

"Yes, señora!" Emily quickly went to change her clothes.

It was Emily who woke the kid up. The kid knew that he is not going to school that day because it is Saturday. At the age of 6, he now knows when to stand or not.

Emily can make the kid follow her. So, Laura ordered her to wake the child up. Because if it were Laura, then the two would definitely argue.

It also took about an hour before they left the mansion. The family was in a white Mercedes Benz except for Luigi.

The kid didn't want to go because his father was not with him. But later, they were able to get Michael to come along. The trip from Rome Termine to Torino was also long. Michael and Emily were in the back of the car. The plan was Emily is in front of the car while Laura is driving. But because Michael insisted that he wanted his Tata next to her, Laura also didn't insist. What matters to Laura is that she can be with the child because her mother wants to see her grandchild who she hasn't seen for so long. But if only Laura rules, she would not let Emily come along because of the sudden change of her style. She used to like Emily but later became a rival to her son Michael, something she couldn't do anything. She is just trying to understand her son.

It also took hours before they reached the gate of Laura's mother's house. Michael and Emily quickly move, but Emily stayed in the car to take care of their cargo.

Emily was the only one who did that. She had no complaints because it was her job. That's all she thought. After that, she helped in the kitchen. People were busy in the kitchen. There were also Filipinos there and two Peruvian housekeepers.

Emily became close to her fellows. Although she knew that Peruvians were kind, it is still a different feeling if you are talking to a fellow Filipino.

Emily couldn't help in the kitchen because Michael didn't do anything but call her because he wanted to be with Emily while playing with other kids. She was just next to Michael, something his mother Laura hated.

Michael paid close attention to her tata, which seemed like a huge sin to Emily. In Michael's actions, he makes her mother jealous, something he has never understood for he was still young.

It was late at night when they reached and returned to Rome. Laura was tired of the long drive. It was Emily who took care of their cargoes in the car. But she took care of the kid first who slept the entire length of the trip.

She carried Michael to his room and arranged him on the bed.

She put on a thick blanket and did not take off the clothes he was wearing. Before getting in the car, she had cleaned the child because he might sleep dirty. Therefore, she made sure that the child was clean in his bed.

Nothing was left in the car. She made sure it was all well and prepared before her Señora Laura could use it the next day. Not satisfied, she even made sure that the car was clean before she entered the mansion.

Even though Emily was very tired, she was still not sleepy. She was thinking about how her boss had badly treated her. She planned to resign and look for another job. But what she was thinking of was Michael, the kid she was taking care of, who she had promised never to leave. She was about to close her eyes when she suddenly heard a loud crash, something that surprised her. She first looked at Michael as if he was awakened by the powerful thing that was thrown to the floor, which she was sure it was from the couple's bedroom. Michael was fast asleep and very tired. Emily fixed his blanket, and slowly, she also covered herself with a blanket. This is a sign that she has no interest in the argument of the two. But over time, she had a different feeling. One of them seemed to be packing his clothes. Emily was worried that the two couples would eventually split up. At that moment, she forgot to close the door. There, she noticed that her lady boss was pulling the suitcase.

"Torno domani per prendere il bambino!" Laura said.

"Non solo si ha diritto al bambino, ho il dirito di, se vi piace Lunedi, Martedì, e voi mercoledi. Per and Giovedi Venerdì Sabato by Domenica.

"Hmph!"

Laura was shocked at her husband's words. She couldn't defend herself because she knew that Luigi had the right as the child's father. She could not take care of Michael alone. And all of their arguments were heard by Emily.

She knew she was going to be stuck between the two rocks. She knew that wherever the child went with one of his parents, she was with him. So the next day, she was preparing herself because she knew Laura would take her with the child. She couldn't do anything because she knew it wasn't easy to find a job. She had to endure with her lady boss.

The next day, her expectation of fetching them with the child came. She had to obey her boss because it would not be easy to leave the child alone if she was used to it. She also promised that she would not leave Michael behind.

"Prendere oggetti personali di Michael ci rimarrà con me per un paio di giorni. Con te?" Laura said.Emily just nodded. She did not longer object to what her boss wishes.

She quickly arranged all the kid's belongings. She made sure he had everything and even her personal belongings. Michael and Emily got in the car. They will temporarily be staying in the new house that

Laura had acquired. It was Emily's first day that she would be in the new house Laura bought for her son Michael. Emily noticed that she has a different feeling when transferring to a new house again. The house is a bit huge, and she is certain that she will be going to clean it.

But that's not what Emily cares about but herself about what could happen to her inside the house. But Emily seems to be safe in cleaning the house. Michael asked her to accompany him to play in the park.

"Tua madre mi rimprovere quando non ho fatto la pulizia de casa!" said Emily.

"I prendo cura di mia mama, a portarla pulire la casa c'è mansion papà. Ci rilascia quelli vengono a compagni di gioco in attesa nel parco!" Michael said.

Emily did not say anything more. She quickly stood up and put on her clothes. She thought she would continue cleaning the house when they came back from Michael's playtime.

She just wished that Laura would not go home early so she wouldn't be scolded. Emily felt worried while Michael was playing with his classmates. It was late in the afternoon, and Emily quickly arranged the house. She was always praying that her boss would not come early. Maybe that will be the first time she would be scolded for not cleaning the rest of the house. When she first heard the couple shouting at each other, she almost didn't want to leave her room in worry that she might be implicated. Her tongue almost fluttered during her period of cleaning. She paused for a moment to rest. Later, she felt the squeaky sound of the door opening. She got up quickly and headed to the kitchen. She pretended to be busy with her kitchen work.

The footsteps were coming closer to her. Emily felt very nervous that her boss might have come.

"The boss wants me to bring you home. Michael will be sleeping at the other house with you, Emily," said driver Arture.

Emily glanced back as she made sure her boss didn't come. She heard a man's voice and certainly not her boss.

"It's you, Arture. You surprised me! I wonder who has come," Emily said surprisingly at Arture's arrival.

"I'm sorry if you were shocked."

"Just a moment. I'll just get dressed, as well as Michael!"

"I'll wait in the car outside the gate. The car might lose!" Arture exclaimed.

Chapter Four

Michael spent almost three days in his mother's place and four days in his father's, Luigi. Emily was in her day-off every Sunday. But sometimes she was given extra pay to take care of the personal belongings of Michael and Luigi if she is needed on Sundays. But often, Luigi personally takes care of his son. The father is helpless when the child always looks for his tata. Came the day that the child is under the care of his father. Luigi finds the child always clean and happy when with her tata Emily whom she also enjoys. It is not difficult to make Michael follow in everything his father wants. Because his tata is beside him, he saw the kindness of his child.

So he wondered why his son is obedient to his tata Emily. The child is obedient and respectful.

He also noticed that the child often prays. He is even at the forefront of the dining table for the prayer before eating.

Luigi is secretly delighted. She thought Emily's parents raised her so well; that's why his son, Michael, had the right attitude. So if Michael was not with him, he knew his son is in good hands even if Michael's mother is there. He is even more confident to Emily in raising his son.

It wasn't hard for Luigi when Emily is there for his son, Michael. Because even when he's in the house working, he can see all of Emily's actions for his son.

He saw his son Michael and Emily get along well with each other. He noticed how Michael shows affection to Emily. Michael was even less likely to call her, Mom. Their frequent play was Emily's only secret to getting the child closer to her.

She did not get tired of serving him. She even treated Michael as her own child. That's one of the things Luigi noticed on Emily even though Luigi was far away.

His son hardly wants to talk to him when he has projects in faraway places. But Luigi is confident that his son Michael will be well taken care of by Emily. So Luigi and Emily often talk on the phone to check on his son Michael.

In those moments, Emily was almost hesitant to talk to her boss, but she has nothing to do with it. Luigi always wanted to check on his son, especially when Luigi was out of town.

Emily always felt shy every time the phone rings.

It's like her heart is beating when she hears the voice of her boss.

But Emily doesn't want Luigi to notice it even though he has a feeling of it. But in the corner of her smile, she realized that she is happy when she is talking to her boss.

Emily doesn't want to tease herself that she has a weird admiration of her boss, something she hadn't dreamed about because she knew her boss had a wife, and that was Laura. She didn't want to have the illusion that her boss would like her because it was unlikely to happen. That's all Emily thought to herself.

Emily only can breathe a sigh of relief when she learned that Michael's dad's phone was down, so she returned to her work.

She felt glad when Luigi was talking to her even though she was not who Luigi needed. But, Emily had the feeling that Luigi was also looking at her. She knew that her boss trusted her when it came to caring for her son, Michael. Until the day came, Michael will go to his mother, Laura. That Monday, Emily felt different. She had heavy feet leading to her boss Laura's house. She felt her heart filled with fear for some unknown reason. She noticed that her boss had a heavy feeling on her. She also saw that Laura is jealous every time the kid kisses Emily, and Laura will just be second, something she doesn't like.

Laura looked differently to Michael when he is approaching her. She wants to avoid the child, but she also loves him. Only a kiss and a hug can relieve her tiredness. The beats in her chest grew stronger. She could not understand herself. Her feet almost didn't want to walk. She felt like she had done a great sin to Laura.

Emily wondered when Laura was at the front door. She just continued walking toward the door. Her eyes widened as she faced the unexpected guest of surprise.

Laura said, "Don't go inside the house anymore. I prepared all your clothes, and someone will replace you. And here's your back pay. I hope you never come back here!"

"Eh, right away? Can I just say goodbye to Michael?" Emily begged.

"For what? Your wages and clothes are there. You do not need to be thankful, nor to say goodbye to my child. That's all you've got. Don't try to come in, and I'll call the police!"

She took the envelope with money, and her clothes were not even arranged. It was just placed in a black garbage bag. Emily felt self-pity.

She was no longer surprised by the reaction of her boss. She was expecting it, so she just turned away and did not bid goodbye to

Michael. At that moment, Emily could not help but weep at how cruel her boss had treated her.

Suddenly, Emily groaned in the middle of the road. She wasn't embarrassed even though she knew people were watching at her. And then she went to her aunt in Vittorio.

It was almost dark when Emily repeated the knock on the door. Aunt Ana, out of her chair, suddenly stood in front of the television. She quickly peered into the hole of who was outside knocking. Then, she was startled by the sight of Emily from the door. Ana opened the door quickly for her niece.

"W-why are you here? It's only Monday, right?" Aunt Ana asked her niece.

"I'm fired from my job!" Emily said sadly in front of her aunt Ana.

"Ha? How did that happen?" asked the aunt.

"I do not know. I don't know!"

"Take a break, and let's talk tomorrow. I noticed you look so tired!"

"All right."

Emily went straight into the bedroom to rest. The reason for her dismissal from work was a big puzzle for Ana.

During those moments, tears wanted to burst from Emily's dim eyes. She couldn't understand herself, and her boss why she did that.

She really wondered about what she had done to her lady boss. But her heart sank when she suddenly left the kid without even saying goodbye.

"I wonder how he is doing," she said to himself.

He already knew Michael's temperament. That won't stop him from crying until he is not next to her. On the other hand, Emily had to be firm despite her sudden dismissal from work.

Emily almost spent a week in the house of her aunt, Ana. She would rather clean the house than go with a walk. No matter how hard her relatives tried to go with them, she couldn't be forced. They were worried that Emily might not do good to herself.

"Why haven't you walked in yet, Aunt Ana? You may miss the mass in Urbana. You will have to wait until 5 pm. Remember, it's the last mass for the morning!" Emily said.

"Aren't you really going to join your cousins?"

"Aunt, I just want to be home alone and lock myself in the room."

"Cousin, are you really not going with mom and with us?" her cousin Novie said.

"All right, if you don't want to come with your cousins and with us, you can just heat something you want to eat there when you're hungry!" said Ana.

"Don't worry, and I'll take care of my food."

Emily kissed Aunt Ana quickly on her cheek. Novie followed right away with her cousins. Then they hurried out the door. Emily twisted the doorknob and made sure it was appropriately locked and cannot be opened easily.

Inside the house, she cleaned first the bed and fixed the beddings along with thick blankets to protect them from cold. As soon as she made sure the bedroom was clean, she followed the bathroom.

Here, she saw the busy inhabitants of Europe. Her cousin's clothes and personal interior were scattered. They have no time to clean. Therefore, she carefully fixed it and put it in a basket of filthy rags.

Her purge was stopped when she got hungry. He temporarily gave up what he was doing. She quickly went to the kitchen and took a korneto from the refrigerators inside. That was her lunch. She did not use to eat rice even though she was still in the Philippines.

Emily really likes bread, especially at night. But she used to eat only at lunch. And this time around, korneto is enough for her.

Emily continued what she was doing. She wearied herself so that she could not think of the child she had left behind in the care of her mother, Laura. But Emily could not keep the boy from his memory. She took care of him for almost seven years. She did not realize that tears were resting on his cheeks.

"How is he doing?" Emily whispered to herself.

Chapter Five

One morning inside Emily's aunt, she did not expect her visitor, Luigi. Even though Emily was surprised, she didn't let anybody notice it.

"Come back home. The kid is looking for you. He won't stop asking me unless you come back home. And from there, he'll return going to his school."

"What about your wife when I get back?" Emily asked her boss directly.

"You know I have a separate house. I don't live with her anymore! You will just come to my house during the day when the child is with me. You're not going to go to my ex-wife."

"I'll think about your offer."

"Please."

Luigi also could not force Emily to return home to look after the kid. So, when he got back, he frustratedly told his son Michael about it.

"I'o vuolio tata? Hu hu hu!" pleaded Michael.

"Sorry my son!"

Michael 's crying in front of his father took so long. So, Luigi could do nothing but bring the kid to the nearest mall. He wished that even at those moments, he would forget his tata Emily.

The father and son were about to go home when Michael suddenly shouted, which made Luigi surprised.

The boy saw his tata Emily walking inside the mall unexpectedly.

"Tata, tata, tata, Emily!" said Michael while running to Emily.

Luigi couldn't oppose more to what his son behaved inside the mall when Michael suddenly embraced Emily. Emily, though shocked, her longing for the child was so intense that she quickly ran to him and hugged him, a sign that she could not hide her longing. At that moment, Luigi approached the two.

"He won't leave you unless you come home to join him. I'm heading to Germany in the next few days. The child loves you so much that he wants you to watch over him."

Emily wept. She did not expect to hear that the child loved her too. So, she quickly embraced it again to let the child feel that she loved him, also. Even if Emily wanted to avoid them, she would make the two take her away because the child held Emily's arms so tight.

"I want to say goodbye to my aunt in Vittorio before we go to your house." Michael heard what she told his father.

It further tightened his grip on Emily.

He didn't let go of her arms as they went to the apartment of Emily's aunt. At that moment, Emily's relatives were amazed at her decision. But what they noticed the most was the child's behavior of not letting go of Emily's hands that made them very happy.

Luigi was just sitting in the living room, waiting for Emily as she was fixing her pieces of stuff that she will bring with her to the mansion. Emily noticed that there was a strange glint in Luigi's eyes. She immediately turned her gaze as her boss was turning his look towards her direction. She noticed a strange glow on her chest. She knew this was impossible, and so, she ordered her chest to restrain the force of her heartbeat. But she felt that the beat and the pulse got stronger.

She tried to hide her feelings to her boss and prayed to hide it forever.

Emily took care of all the child's needs. Although Luigi was far away, he knew that Emily would take good care of his son, Michael.

Luigi had great trust for Emily as his child's nanny.

It took him almost three weeks in Germany for his commitment to work. Even remotely, it was the only cellphone call to find out what was going on with his son and his nanny, Emily. Even in the school assignments of the child, Michael could easily teach Michael through 'Viber.' So, there was no doubt that even when the father is far away, they are still in touch. Emily secretly smiled at the father. She looked at them like they are just friends. She temporarily left them while talking to Viber. Emily went to the kitchen to prepare snacks for Michael. After serving the snack, she returned to the kitchen and continued the cleanup.

It also took some time before her work was finished. She rested next to Michael when she was tired until Saturday night came again.

Emily would be forced to take Michael to his mother. Even though she didn't want to see Laura, she couldn't do anything. That's what Luigi ordered. Emily had to bring Michael to her mother's place until Luigi had not returned from Germany.

Emily's knees shook as they approached the door of Laura's house. But she decided to be firm in front of Laura. She just thought that it wasn't Laura who took her, but Luigi.

So, Emily knew that she had nothing to do with Luigi's decision even though they agreed before that she will not bring Michael to Laura's place anymore.

Also, the supposed nanny of Michael at Laura's home suddenly returned to the Philippines.

Emily pressed the buzzer at the door of Laura's house. She assured herself that she was firm and that she already knew what to answer the moment Laura will ask her questions. Even she was nervous, she still forced herself to stand firm in front of Laura.

A creaking sound was slightly produced by the large door. The new housemaid opened the door and let Michael enter. Emily's chest loosened. The shock and fear in her chest disappeared as she saw another person, and not Laura opened the door.

After all, she doesn't have to be afraid of the one who became once her boss.

"Maybe I am just thinking about respect," was what Emily had said to herself. She would still have the respect of his boss, Luigi's wife, even though they were no longer together and their wedding was not yet annulled.

At Luigi's house, Monday, she did not expect his guest, Laura.

"Why did you bring Emily back here to take care of the child?!"

"I got her, and I am the one who is paying her, so you're out there!"

"I hate her, get rid of her!"

"You have a new helper, don't you?"

"I don't want her for Michael to take care of him!"

"You ask Michael, and he made Emily back!"

"You can give whatever he wants!"

"I'm just following the boy's wishes!"

"I'll get her out!"

"You're up!"

It was Luigi who first to walk out.

"Whatever you do, I'll take her away!" Laura said angrily.

In front of their house, Laura was waiting. She knew it was Saturday, and Emily would bring Michael to her mansion. Then, Laura met Emily.

"Luigi and I have talked about that this is your last day of bringing the child here!"

"Señorito didn't say anything like that to me," Emily said.

"Alright, I let you know that I'm Michael's mother, and I decide who wants to be with my son."

"You're not the one I'm talking to. I'll just go when Señorito Luigi says it!" Emily turned away. She never gave her former boss the chance to speak again.

"That's rude!"

Laura noticed that Emily was fighting. She felt insulted by Emily's behavior. If she only had the power to burn Emily with her eyes, she would have done it so. She couldn't accept what a nanny had done to her that measured her personality.

"Hmp! Let's see what you can do to me when you lose in my way!"

Laura's eyes sharpened when she stared at Emily. But she kept her emotions under control to her female rival to his son, Michael.

Luigi returned to Germany for his contract as an architect. It took him several months without going back home.

It was during those times that Laura, without Luigi's knowledge, would get rid of Emily as Michael's nanny.

Laura was at the door of Luigi's house, waiting for Emily to arrive. She never expected that day to happen.

"You are just until there, and you can no longer enter the house!"

"This is the house of my boss who pays me, and so I won't leave."

"You forget that our marriage has not yet been annulled even though I am separated from him. So, I know where I stand in this house!" Laura said angrily to Emily.

"You, what are you here?" In those moments, Michael could see how his mother would talk to her tata Emily. He could do nothing but cry and run to his room. Emily's shoulders fell again from insults and unreasonable words of Laura.

Chapter Six

Since Emily was no longer in Michael's eyes, his behavior changed. He would not eat at the right time, and he was difficult to wake in the morning. Michael had become a headache to Laura, something for which her patience was losing. Even in the classroom, the child's manner could not be controlled. It made a big problem for Luigi. But Luigi's great patience for the son was still there.

"Why is it that you have trouble in class, and you are not studying? What do you want?" asked his father.

"I'o Voglio, tata!"

"Tata? No, io Voglio tata!" Michael quickly ran to his room and shut up. Luigi could do nothing for what his son wanted.

Luigi had difficulty deciding. Although he was the one who pays for Emily, his ex-wife's decision would still be followed when it comes to their child. Luigi once confronted his ex-wife, but Laura remained adamant that Luigi wanted Emily back to take care of the child.

"No way! Find another one. That child will also get tired looking for his tata. He will get tired! Just let him cry!" The child no longer entered the school and never woke up early in the morning. He would not even play with his cousins.

"Do you know why I get rid of your 'ragazza'? Because I know you like her!" Laura said.

"Why is the topic about me? What we are talking about are the kid and his tata. Why me?"

"Why don't you admit that you have a secret admiration at that woman?!"

"What?!"

"Why can't you speak now?" Laura said repeatedly.

"When you got in touch with your producer, I let you go. I thought you were having fun! And you know we're done.

If I bring Emily back to care for Michael, it is because of our kid's upbringing. My feelings are out of this.

Emily is like a real mother than you!" Luigi turned his back before Laura.

Luigi's ex-wife just stared at what Luigi told her. She didn't expect Luigi to hear all that. Luigi also thought about what Laura said. How could he love a woman who only shows good things? Like how she was taking care of Michael. The child was always well-behaved, respectful, and had cared for learning. Even at such a young age, he already knew his responsibilities as a student that made Luigi very happy as a father. He could learn all things quickly, including prayer and giving gratitude for food.

Luigi suddenly smiled at what he remembered. He had a strange feeling every time he heard Emily's voice when he was calling from

Germany. He felt different energy. All he knew was he was happy when he could listen to the lady's voice.

Luigi smiled secretly. Even himself, he did not realize that this was how he felt towards his child's nanny.

"Is that why?" Luigi said to himself. His lips just came out with a smile. "Am I in love with Emily?" he whispered to himself.

"Is that why my heart smiles when I hear her voice from my call from Germany?"

Luigi was amazed at himself. Luigi wondered how he could bring Emily back for her son, Michael.

"I'm going to their house in Piazza Vittorio. I will encourage her to come back to this house!" That was all Luigi thought when he was in the car.

There was no guarantee that she would give another chance if he again once asked Emily to return home to take care of the child personally. But Luigi suddenly spotted someone outside his car, Laura. He saw his ex-wife went inside a restaurant.

"Liar! She said she has nothing to do with that producer!" Luigi paused for a moment on one side.

"Anyway, we're done! I don't care who you date," Luigi said. He thought of following his wife to make sure they were what he saw. But he did not follow his wife inside the restaurant. Instead, he waited patiently in his car for several hours. He hid so Laura would not notice that her husband was following her.

But Luigi was bored. He was about to start his car's engine when Laura and the producer jumped out of the restaurant. Luigi planned to never get out of the car, and just follow them wherever they were going. Luigi's eyes were sharp, though the vehicle he was following did some overtakes, he managed to catch up quickly.

He was devastated when he saw that car enter a motel. He quickly took the picture and even the plate number of the car they were riding.

He created a way for him to follow his wife without her knowledge. Even at the motel, he was able to bribe the attendant, so he could come in and ask for the motel's video file.

The attendant initially refused to allow him to carry out his plans. But the money was big enough to have the attendant's approval.

His plan of going to Emily's place in Piazza Vittorio did not push through because he put everything that he witnessed at that moment first. For him, everything was done between them as husband and wife. But on the other hand, Laura would continue to say that she was still entitled to marriage even though they were separated from the house. So, he did one thing to stop Laura's madness that Luigi wasn't doing anything wrong.

"She probably doesn't have anything here. It is the answer to her speaking out of turn!" Luigi said to himself. He prepared himself for everything, even as they exited the restaurant and hotel they had left.

Luigi did not return to Germany first. He took care of his son, Michael. He could only insist on Michael when he cares about him or does the bathing of the child. He took care of the child as he used to see from Emily.

He also used to bring Michael to school personally. Luigi saw what Emily has to offer for Michael. So, it is no wonder that the child is so close to Emily. She considered him her son.

Laura, on the other hand, had no interest in her son, Michael. Everything was up to Emily.

Luigi had an emergency call from Germany. He had to come back for his job. Despite his will, he could do nothing. He was forced to look for a babysitter.

But all who applied did not pass the child's taste. Whoever they present to the child, his mouth always uttered his tata, Emily. So even though Michael's father did not want to go to Germany, it did not stop his son's desire to let the person who up brought him return to their house.

Luigi's legs were heavy towards the direction of Emily's house. Again, he pleaded that she would take care of his child again. With no definitive answer to Emily's decision, Luigi thought Michael would answer all her questions and concerns.

Suddenly there was a knock on the door, and Emily opened it immediately. The lady was speechless when Michael suddenly hugged her.

He was filled with longing for Emily, who surprised her. He even kissed her many times on her cheek.

Emily suddenly asked them to go inside the house. Michael immediately sat down on the couch and embraced the young lady again that made Emily felt even more excitement to him.

"You love tata, ah!"

The boy nodded and kissed Emily's cheek even more. The kid asked to go outside with Emily. The child did not leave her side, which made the young lady unable to change her clothes. During those moments, Michael's dad was just shaking his head.

He no longer had difficulty in granting the child's request. Emily noticed that she followed him through everything the boy wanted to do with him, especially when he was taken to the mall.

Emily was glad because she noticed that the child was happy with her. When the child got tired, they went to Michael's favorite fast-food chain. The kid chose the fast-food chain. The three of them waited for a while for their order. So, Luigi had the opportunity to leave the child with her.

Emily was clueless. Although she did not want to agree, he quickly handed the key to the house and the money they would use for the budget. Then, Luigi promptly stood up.

When Luigi was about to leave, he noticed that his son was not chasing him, a sign that the boy wanted to be with Emily. He saw the child was happy with Emily, which he secretly liked.

"When Emily returns, I know the kid will be happy," Luigi told himself.

Luigi only used trains going to Germany that was covered by the European Schengen. It was what he used to ride if not going to America and Canada. Here, he could see the vine and apple farms stretching to the edge of the railroad. It was what gives him so much fun in those moments.

Chapter Seven

In Germany, even when he was at work, his mind was far away from what he was thinking, aside from his son. He couldn't take away from his mind the whole of Emily's face. A smile on his cheek drew the pleasure that was making him happy.

"When I get home, you have a second mommy, child!" that's all Luigi said to himself. It was near him where he was standing inside the building that the foundations suddenly gave way and collapsed. He was stuck by it.

"Eeeeee!" shouted Luigi.

"Señorito?!" shouted by a shocked worker there.

They were all unprepared for that event. They were in danger. With the heavy weight of steel that fell to his knees, Luigi lost consciousness. He didn't even know what was going on in his surroundings.

Michael's father was rushed to the nearest hospital. Luigi was also unconscious for some time, and this worried by the company owned by his family.

Luigi was in the hospital for a few days, and he still couldn't believe what happened to him.

"Noooooooo!" Luigi shouted as he realized that one of his legs was cut off.

Everybody around him was so supportive of him so that it would somehow lighten the burden of his heart.

But what made his mind more troubled was when he remembered his son and Emily. He asked himself if how well they were doing. Would he still be accepted despite what happened to him? Would Emily still love him as he already knew to himself that he's already in love to her? How could he tell how he feels if his one leg was cut off?

"I'm just going to be a burden to her! Hmp!" that's all Luigi said. "It's crazy that Emily will love me, madness!"

He held a bottle of Vodka, no lemon, no salt that would serve as a safeguard to his taste. He wanted to drown himself in the wine because he couldn't accept himself now.

In those moments, Luigi's best friend Miguel, a German, was there.

"It's not about your manhood, your diploma, or what you know when it comes to drawing up a plan. You can still even face the cruel challenges of life. Life is important if your son, Michael, is important to you. There is no reason why you should not continue the life you are enjoying today," says Miguel.

"How can I face my family, my children, if this is my situation? I don't want them to pity me!" Luigi strongly told Miguel.

"Don't pity yourself. We can do something about that, and I know you'll be happy about it!" Luigi did not say anymore, and he had just let Miguel decide.

'Prosthetic leg' was put on for Luigi to walk. It was difficult to accept his situation, and he could do nothing, so he didn't decide anymore for that matter. He knew he was just pitying himself and didn't want to imprison himself for his weaknesses. Miguel trained Luigi to walk. No matter how hard he had to walk like nothing had happened to him. Luigi had to hide everything that happened to him, so it took him almost a year. He needed to do that. Luigi was filled with longing for his son to hug. He tried to achieve all these things just right after his foot surgery.

He felt contented as he talked to his son over Viber. He only wondered why Emily didn't even take a peek at Viber, where he was talking to his son, Michael. Though he was pulled from his sadness, he thought at one point he would suddenly visit Emily's house in Piazza Vittorio. There he planned to confess what is inside of his heart. Here, he felt that this woman also was falling in love with him. He was just smiling because he was fooling himself that nothing had happened to him. He was convincing himself that he was still normal to this day. In fact, he's just doing it for his son, Michael, and if it's lucky, Emily will welcome him.

He would probably be the happiest man in the world, even though the truth was just a dream.

He did the right thing. He would deal with what had happened to him and would tell his son about it. It was sure that he wouldn't show this to his ex-wife, Laura, because he knew she would just say bad things to him if she would know what happened to him.

So, he decided to call Emily's number. He wanted to give her an appreciation and to make her feel that he was ready to court her.

"R-ringgggggggggggggggg!" He repeatedly called Emily's number, but no one answered the other line,

something he worried about on. He even repeated the call to Emily's cellphone.

"She doesn't answer, so why?" Luigi said to himself.

He tried to call his son on Viber. Michael was on the other side. But he did not pursue his purpose to know where Emily was. He noticed that Laura was behind Michael.

He just talked to his son, Michael. They also had a one-hour conversation. And after that, Luigi said goodbye.

In his room, Luigi was lying in bed. It was still a puzzle to him about Emily not even took a peek at Viber, something she used to do also for a while. But now there was none even a glance. That was what he was most wondered about.

Luigi thought Laura had something to do with the incident. He felt that she might get rid of the poor tata. Because of this, he decided to go home. Fortunately, he could walk well, and so, no one might notice that his original leg was gone.

From Germany, he was carrying the roses he had bought and the chocolate that his son, Michael, had requested. Little did Michael know that his father was coming home. One year later, the boy just thought that his father was busy at work in Germany as an architect.

"My son will be so happy with his requested chocolate that I bought!" His sweet smile fluttered to the corner of his lips. At the same time, he thought of how he was going to face Emily. Luigi was in Rome. He first went to his house here in Parioli but his son Michael was not there, and Emily was not there, too. He thought that Emily might have taken the child to the park because it was the child's interest.

Michael used to play games with his fellow kids.

Luigi did not wish to wait for the two, but he fixed his eyes upon the television until the night was deep, and the two had not yet returned home. He was about to leave the house when the phone rang. He thought Laura was on the other line.

"Hello?!" Luigi replied.

"Hello, Luigi? It's your mom! " answered Maria, Luigi's mom.

"Oh, Mom! What made you call?"

"I was just trying to call at your house."

"Why?!"

"Michael, your son, is always crying, and Emily is gone," Maria explained to Luigi's son.

"What happened to Michael? What happened to my child?!" Luigi asked worriedly.

"Because Emily is in prison. Laura put Michael's tata into jail!"

"Haa?! How did that happen?"

"I do not know. It's best to go to the hearing tomorrow so you can visit Emily, too."

"I'm confused, Mom. I can't understand how that happened!" wondered Luigi. But Luigi was unaware that their conversation had ended.

Luigi was suddenly perplexed by what his mother, Maria, said.

He calmed down first and continued to think why Emily was imprisoned and in what case Laura filed suit against her.

He did not realize that he had been in Germany for so long. He also didn't come home for a long time.

"Thanks to my friend, who took care of me. If not because of him, I might be dead, and I will never see my son Michael again," Luigi said to himself.

The next day, his mind was full of questions about how he would start everything. During his time in Germany, he did not know how to explain his experiences.

On the other hand, it was better to keep everything secret about what happened to him so that Laura would not start asking more questions. What was essential to him during those times was to prepare himself for the issues that troubled his mind.

In the hallway, the two, Laura and Luigi, were not expected to face each other. The emotions of both sides were controlled because Michael was there. In those moments, Michael suddenly ran into his dad, something Luigi had been hoping for. Laura had just looked at the child's behavior. Luigi immediately noticed that Laura was with a man but didn't pay much attention to him. It was easy to register in his mind that it was Laura's ex who he saw at the motel before.

Luigi also quickly noticed that Michael has a new nanny, a Peruvian. The babysitter has a small, lean body. Luigi promptly turned his gaze away to the new nanny.

Laura ordered Michael's new nanny, Lengleng, to move the child away, and she will just talk to Luigi. Lengleng quickly acted even though she could not understand English and Italian. She quickly realized what Laura wanted to do.

"You're gone for so long! I don't know what happened to you in Germany," Laura said angrily.

Luigi just changed the things he was about to say.

"I wasn't allowed to come back here immediately. The jobs that I have been waiting for have been terminated," Luigi explained.

"Or, you might have meant to never show to me again so you could have the kid and be right to him!" Luigi changed her look from Laura's. "I don't understand why Emily is in jail, and why we are in court!"

"Because she kidnapped my son Michael, and she belongs to it!"

"Indeed, up to this day, you are angry with her! You didn't even give her a chance to defend herself! "

"That's all right with her! She is a thief of love!"

"Hmp!"

It was Luigi who withdrew from their dispute. He knew their conversation would yield no sense.

"I know you're going to back out of the fight because you know you even engage to your kid's nanny!"

Luigi stopped listening to Laura after making false accusations that were not good in his ears. He hurried to walk without hearing what he was saying. Laura's face was filled with sadness over Luigi's actions. She was still talking when Luigi turned his back to her, something Laura didn't like.

Chapter Eight

In the courtroom, everyone was holding back their breaths. Even Luigi didn't know what to do. He could do nothing but sympathize with Emily's condition when he saw her entered the courtroom handcuffed. But Luigi tried to be calm in court. He just thought Emily had to win the case. Luigi was surprised when his son Michael was requested by the court to sit in the witness stand. They let the boy in their manner explained what others say about him being kidnapped.

"Where did your nanny take you when your Mommy and Daddy weren't with you?" the lawyer asked the child.

"At their home in Vittorio, while tata used to go to her work," the boy replied to the lawyer.

"Eh, you do have money, right, for your expense that your Daddy left to your nanny?"

"If Daddy has money left for us, why does my nanny have to work outside just to buy our food?"

"Does Mommy have no money left for you?"

"She was gone for a long time. She's gone longer than Daddy!"

"Is your nanny beating you?"

"No. Tata is kind to me. And even though I'm naughty, she doesn't beat me. If I saw her not talking, I knew she was angry with me. I'm going to stop what I'm doing!"

"What are you doing?"

"Playing!"

"Are you eating well?"

"When she's done cooking, she will prepare the food, and she will feed me. Then she will freshen me up before going to bed at night. We're just two."

Luigi was impressed by his son's response to the questions. He let the child explain what happened to them during the time that he was not with Michael. In those moments, Luigi couldn't help but look at Laura's side. He noticed that his ex-wife was angry. The court found almost no holes in filing a lawsuit against his nanny, Emily.

There was one last question to the child. "If you are going to choose, to whom do you want to go with your mom or your dad?"

The boy was suddenly saddened by not mentioning his nanny in the choices. Michael was temporarily silent. Suddenly the boy wept, stood, and ran to his nanny. It was not to expected that they will be treated by Michael in court.

"I want my nanny! I'll just go with Yaya Emily! I don't want mommy!"

Everyone was shocked at their unexpected moment. Laura's forehead deepened to what Michael did.

Even the Judge was shocked and said, "Mrs. Laura Casalino-Bandini, you filed a lawsuit against your child's nanny. He doesn't want to come even to you or your spouse. To whom does the child's nanny is staying with?"

From the chair, Luigi shouted.

"She is staying at my place. For a long time, she is the one who takes care of my son. Emily is the tata of my son," said Luigi. "And for a long time, I was gone, I was in the hospital recovering."

In the courtroom, Luigi was not ashamed to break his pants to show that his left leg was no longer original. He also had all the medical records to prove he had an accident while in control of the building.

"Then, where the child is, the nanny should be there and will stay in your control, Mr. Luigi Bandini."

That was the court's order. Luigi's smile deepened at the unexpected decision of the court over whom the child was going.

There was no case against Emily for saying she kidnapped the child. The child stated that no kidnapping occurred. The court also confirmed that Emily looked for a living to feed Michael for almost a year when Luigi and Laura suddenly disappeared. Emily acted as the parent of the child when they were not there when the child needed food, clothing, and care. The child testified in court, and Emily was found not guilty.

Laura became even angrier that she no longer had the right to care for Michael.

"No!" Laura shouted in the courtroom once, and the Judge slammed his wooden hammer on his desk. The judge got up and left. Everyone was surprised by the court's decision except Laura.

Luigi approached Laura.

"This is a huge insult to me!" Laura growled to Luigi.

"The court has decided. There is nothing I can do in the court decision for our son Michael."

Laura's head grew hot to what Michael said in the court. The boy immediately ran to his nanny, something Laura didn't like. So, Laura decided to leave the courtroom. Even though they were in the hallway, Laura still couldn't stop her mouth.

Laura was with Umberto, who was said to be her live-in partner today. Umberto used to own a famous five-star hotel in Rome.

"I will not allow that the child will not be returned to me!" Laura retorted.

"Let the child go with them. There'll come a time that he will come to you when he grows up," Umberto said.

"Ahh, I won't stop them!"

At that moment, Umberto just sighed to what Laura wanted for her son, Michael. Umberto just looked away and let his partner do her thing until they reached their car in the parking area. Umberto opened the door quickly for Laura.

Luigi, Michael, and also Emily remained inside the court. Luigi's face lit up with a huge smile.

"Dad, you know when you were away, Yaya Emily also worked because she didn't have any money for our expenses. Mommy is in America, too. She stayed there for long, so Yaya Emily didn't know where to get our food."

Luigi smiled at Emily's concern for her son. Luigi glanced at Emily, something she hadn't expected in those moments.

"Thank you, and you're there. You didn't leave my son alone," Luigi said.

"I love your son. I took care of him since he was a baby. The more he stayed with me, the more he loved me.

It's hard for me to be away from the kid. His life seemed like an extension of my life. So, I might suffer if I will lose him."

"I will not lose you, Tata, because I love you!"

Emily just gave Michael a sweet smile and embraced the child. In those moments, Luigi was just staring. He noticed that the two were like mother and son. The happiness that Luigi felt was different. He thought that for almost a year that he had disappeared, Emily had suffered a lot of pain in Laura's hand.

"During the long time that I've been gone, many things have happened. I didn't expect Laura will do that to Emily. No one even knew that I had an accident in Germany.

If I stayed there longer, Laura might have put Emily to jail," Luigi told himself.

In those moments, he looked at Emily and was impressed with the girl.

"Sorry, Emily. For a year, I didn't know you went through so much pain in Laura's hand."

"What happened to you, Papa? Why didn't you come back to Italy for so long? And you look skinny? Didn't you eat anything there?" asked Michael in succession.

"I wasn't sent back to Rome right away because we had a big project to finish!"

"But why you didn't just call at home? You used to call, and then you'll look for me," the boy said to the father.

"I just have to finish everything I do there!"

"No. You said before the court that you had an accident. What happened to you? Was that the reason for not returning to Rome immediately?"

The father didn't speak. He just saw his son Michael as wise.

"Maybe you don't love me anymore?" the boy said sadly to the father.

In those moments, Emily was just looking at them. Emily had secret glances to Luigi, and Luigi could immediately catch Emily glaring at him.

"Are you the only one who misses me?" Luigi then looked at Emily's side.

By that time, Michael fell asleep in the middle of chit chat while he was in his father's lap. Luigi slowly lifted Michael and then stood up towards his room. Emily just looked at Luigi's action. Later, Luigi quickly returned to the living room to continue chatting with Emily.

"Thank you for caring for my son. I apologize for Laura's actions. If there's something that happened to you because of Laura, I would never be able to forgive myself."

"What matters is that the court agreed with me. Although she filed a lawsuit, it was proven that I am innocent, and of course, it is based on your child's explanation as he was being questioned.

Michael is smart. He got it from you!"

"Thanks!"

"Sir, I want to have a leave of absence this weekend. I haven't been home for a long time, and my parents maybe are worried that they still can't reach me because of the situation."

"It's up to you, but please come back, and I'll wait for you here."

"I'm not sure if I'm coming back!"

"Why? Is it because of what happened to you while I was away?"

"It isn't easy for my parents about what happened to me. It is difficult for them, and especially they are far from me.

It is also difficult for me to know that they were not in good condition when I was in prison."

"Sorry! When is your plan?" Luigi asked sadly.

"Tonight."

"Huh?!"

Emily just bowed her head in front of Luigi.

"Why tonight? Aren't you going to say goodbye to the kid?"

"It's hard for me to say goodbye while he's here next to me. Maybe he will just stop me."

"We'll have a hard time if you leave," Luigi said.

"Sorry!"

Emily had already carried her bag containing some pieces of stuff. In those moments, Luigi felt a different kind of sadness. But he couldn't do anything. He could see Emily holding tightly her small bag containing her belongings.

"Hope you'll come back, Emily."

Until Emily disappeared, Luigi wrapped himself in sadness. He felt a secret love for the girl who cared for her son Michael.

"How can I explain this to Michael? I might have a hard time because of her sudden leave. Perhaps, tomorrow I will visit her at her place in Vittorio with her relatives. I will make him come back to Rome again!"

Although he knew that Emily had already left last night, Luigi was still looking for luck. He thought Emily was just joking about what she had been told, so he decided to go to Emily the next day at their apartment in Vittorio.

Chapter Nine

At eight o'clock in the morning, Alexandra angrily went to the door to see who had come.

"Good Morning! Emily, is she there?" asked Luigi.

"Yesterday she left for the Philippines," said Alexandra.

"When will she be back here in Rome?"

"She'll never come back here!"

Luigi was stunned. He didn't expect to hear those words from Emily's cousin. Luigi left disappointed. His biggest problem was how he would explain to his son that Emily was already in the Philippines.

The child's longing for the good news was laced with tears. He couldn't stop the child from crying. The boy then turned and went to his room. Luigi dropped a deep breath at the boy's behavior, but he just let him be alone in his bedroom. Then, there was an hour before he would peep if he had stopped crying, and if he was no longer looking for his nanny. But it was already dark, and the boy still didn't show up. Michael ignored even the new maid in the house. She knocked so many times on the door, something to Luigi's wonder and concern. Luigi knocked on the room himself, but Michael still didn't open the door. So, he quickly grabbed the duplicate copy of the key for him to open the door.

"Son?!" asked Luigi.

Slowly, the father approached his child's bed. He thought the child fell asleep from crying. He would have turned away when he heard a small cry. He immediately looked at the child's face. Luigi was so moved when he saw Michael crying. So, he picked him up and hugged the child tightly.

"Do you want to be with your nanny?"

The boy just nodded and let out a small smile, something that made Luigi down. Luigi smiled again and gave his son, Michael a hug. At the Fiumicino Airport, the child could not draw his happiness when he learned that they were heading to the Philippines to visit his nanny. That's what Luigi noticed in his son.

"Papa, how far is the Philippines?"

"It is how long you sleep. So, when you get inside the plane, you go to sleep. Then, when you wake up, we are at the Philippine airport."

"Really?!" the child asked eagerly.

Arriving inside the plane, Michael immediately peered out the window. His seat was next to the window, and he was beside his father, Luigi.

After observing the vast expanse of clouds, Michael quickly fell asleep during the eight-hour wait that his father said to him. Luigi promptly took off his jacket and wrapped it around the boy.

It was early morning when the plane landed. Luigi had just woken up his son even before they had landed.

"Are we here, Papa?" the boy asked the father.

"Yes, we're here, and we're about to get off the plane," Luigi told the son.

At that moment, Michael again looked out the window of the plane. That only made him smile when he woke up, and he felt he was in the Philippines.

After that, they took a bus to Pampanga. It also took them a long time before they reached their destination. Darkness had overtaken them, but it still seemed uncertain whether he was knocking on the right door. During the length of their trip, Michael had just fallen asleep on his father's shoulders. The door still didn't open, so Luigi knocked again. When the door opened...

"L-Luigi, I mean, Señorito?"

Emily was surprised. She did not expect them to come, which made her lost her mind. In those moments, Michael woke up from sleeping on dad's shoulder. Emily was speechless when Michael suddenly hugged her and tried to **grab her neck. She could do nothing but hug him tightly, too. Even her, she felt the excitement for the boy.**

Luigi's big smile brightened as he saw his son's joy.

"Let's sleep together!" Michael leaned over in her lap.

"All right, let's go," Emily said.

They quickly entered the house.

Luigi noted that the house's surroundings were made of bamboo knit-work, and the chairs were also made of bamboo, while the table that they use for dining was made of sawdust.

Even if the house was lightweight, it was considered clean and cool to the eye. Luigi liked it right away. The bathroom was made of stone, and the floor was made of marble. Nor will they be caught up in modern equipment.

Luigi was in awe of what he witnessed.

"I'll be with the boy. That's your child's sweet request. You'll be in the other room. It is only used 'when we have guests, and it has its bathroom."

"Your house is beautiful! Only now have I seen a kind of house like this, old-fashioned but elegant."

"Thanks!"

Luigi then entered his room while Michael was in Emily's room. And Emily's other siblings were with their parents.

At that moment, Emily was secretly pleased. She did not expect the arrival of her guests. Her sadness diminished as she was next to the child who she almost raised. But, was that a smile only for the child?

"For whom really does that beautiful smile?" Emily said to herself.

Emily quickly went into their room with Michael. But still, many questions were bothering her mind, something that made her smile even more. In the morning, with the cockcrowing, Delfin, Emily's father, awoke. Delfin quickly headed to the kitchen to make a tea from avocado leaves. That's what he often drinks every morning. After drinking, he would pull out the carabao rope and would quickly take it to the farm just behind their house. After a few hours, he then quickly searched for the ax to cut wood used for cooking. That's what the old folks used to do. For him, it was a good workout for his body. Delfin was unaware that they had a guest. Perhaps in the substantial woodwork, he was unaware that it created noise.

At that moment, Luigi quickly peeked out the window because of the noise outside the house. He saw a man chopping wood with an ax.

"Buon giorno!" greeted Luigi.

"Who are you?!" Delfin was shocked, and he was about to throw the ax.

"Haa!" Luigi was shocked, too, when he saw the older man holding the ax tightly.

"You're a thief!"

Delfin would have killed Luigi. Fortunately, Emily woke up immediately due to the noise outside.

She couldn't understand why it was so loud, so she came out so fast.

When Delfin was about to hit Emily's visitor...

"Dad, don't! He is my visitor!"

"Ha?!"

"He is my visitor. It was late at night when he came, so I didn't wake you up. You didn't notice his arrival."

"Even though! You should have wakened me up because it's not so easy to trust right away," said Delfin.

Then, it quickly registered in his mind that the guy has a different color. He also noticed that the guy was a foreigner.

"What's his purpose here?"

"The kid just wanted to see me, so they came here," Emily replied.

"You believed then that the reason is the kid and not him!" suddenly yelled Delfin. Then, he went inside the house. Delfin didn't ask anymore. This surprised Emily.

Emily later followed her father to the well to get water to clean the pig's pen.

"Get that out of here, right now!"

"Dad! Señor Luigi and his son will be here only for a few days!"

"You have to think about his wife and why you have been in prison for almost a year!"

"He used to be his wife! And he has nothing to do with what his ex-wife did to me."

"That's the point! He has done nothing for you while you were almost a year in jail!" her father yelled at her.

"But, Dad!"

"My ax is still sharp. If you don't tell him to go home, I'll let my ax to make him go."

Emily was stunned and could no longer break her father's decision. She could do nothing but talk to her ex-Italian boss. So, at the same time, as the child was awake, Luigi and Michael left.

They went through the field embankments that serve their way. They were in the middle of the field, that's why they couldn't do anything even though they slipped almost all the time. That was what Emily immediately noticed when Luigi and Michael arrived late one midnight. And it was something she had been worried about.

Until they reached the road that will take them to Manila, they looked for a place to spend for that night. Then, they plan to stay for just a few days in the Philippines. And after that, they will return to Italy immediately, with the great disappointment of seeing Emily longer.

Even though he knew the boy was crying, Luigi could do nothing. By the time they reached Cubao, Michael had been starving, so they quickly went to the nearest restaurant to quench the child's hunger. As they were eating at their table, Luigi was unaware that a foreigner had been forced to get their bag. They had no chance of knowing that that American executed the plan.

When Luigi was about to pay what they ate, he was shocked when he learned that their bag was gone, which was just placed almost at his feet. They could not do anything but to give his watch as payment. Luigi's mind was drenched. He was worried because all the documents and money were in the bag that was taken. They did not even know

 Arnold G. Ramos

where their feet were going. They went for a walk until they realized that they had gone a long way until an older woman passed by and noticed Michael was crying.

"Why are you crying?"

"I'o fame!"

"Ah, Italiano!"

"Ci!"

"Allora, what happened?"

"Someone snatched my bag!"

The older woman was worried. Been from Italy, she knew the behavior of people there.

"How many days have you been not eating?"

"It's been three days!"

"Haa?! Would you like to stay at my house for a while?

"Can we?"

Luigi's big smile returned. Even though the boy was unaware of what was happening around him, they took a bus ride back to the province. Though Luigi was wondering, he chose to be silent.

He became familiar with the place they were going to. He was even more nervous when he saw that cottage he had just slept one night, the house of Emily.

Luigi was stunned. Who was the woman who rescued them? What was her relationship with the people on that house who forcibly wanted him to be out? Until they reached the house. Delfin saw the returning guest.

"You again?" Delfin would have picked up the bolo that was on the side of the house.

Delfin's eyes widened as he rushed to Luigi. Luigi hid behind the older woman, Amelia.

"Wait a minute! Do you know each other?"

"That's Emily's guest. He's been here in the Philippines for a few days!"

"Brother, be calm first. So far, they lost their money.

Let's shelter them for a while," said Amelia. Delfin was shocked at his sister's decision.

In those moments, Emily watched the three talk with Michael, held by Luigi. But Luigi quickly struggled himself and walked into the house when he noticed that Emily was staring out the window, something that excited the child. From inside the house looking out of the window, Emily quickly moved to face the child approaching her. Luigi was surprised at the child's behavior, something he admired for Emily's warm welcome to his child.

After that, Delfin and Amelia quickly got inside the house, too. They saw Luigi and Michael in the kitchen. It could be seen that they have been eating poorly for a few days, something that Delfin felt sorry for. But as a father, he still couldn't resist speaking in front of Luigi.

"We have only one thing — honor, to be proud of. We are poor, but we fight the challenges of life. So, it would be painful for me to repeat what happened to Emily in Italy!" Delfin said and turned then his back.

In those moments, Emily wanted to stop her father.

"That's enough, Dad! Luigi is not the cause of everything," Emily said.

"It hurts so much to think about Italy, that we could have helped our daughter, Emily!" Luigi was silent on the lady's father's words.

Then, Delfin entered the room. He didn't realize that his sister Amelia was after him.

"Emily's guests may not feel comfortable if you do not stop your anger," said Amelia.

"You can't get rid of what happened to my daughter!"

"I understand, but her problem in Italy was over!"

At that moment, Delfin stared out the window. Still, his sister, Amelia, followed him.

"You cannot blame me. It was difficult for me to know about Emily's bad experiences in Italy. So, it's not that easy for me to just accept it as though no nightmare came to your niece!"

"What matters now is that the problem is over, and Emily has no more problem."

"There is more!"

"Ha?!"

"What is that guy doing here?"

Amelia suddenly became quiet. What would Luigi do at Emily's house? While he already said goodbye, even though his arrival from Italy was uncertain. Swiftly, a smile spread across Amelia's lips, with teasing smiles.

`The next day, the rooster suddenly cried that had been sitting on the guava tree, a sign that it was early morning. There, Delfin would rise to serve coffee made of burnt rice and topped with red sugar. He was about to sip the hot coffee when he suddenly heard something as if someone was cutting woods outside of the house. Delfin wondered because whenever their neighbor would cut woods, it would not be heard since it was far from their home. It made him think significantly about

what he heard. So, Delfin quickly headed outside to find out who was cutting the wood. He was surprised when he saw their visitor, Luigi, was cutting woods, something that made him shocked at that never expected moment.

"Why are you cutting those woods? You're a visitor here!" said Delfin.

"I just want to perspire!"

"Are you sure?"

"Yes, sir!"

The older man left, but in a few minutes, he returned with another cup of coffee. He quickly handed it to Luigi. Although Luigi was not accustomed to burnt rice for coffee, he accepted it wholeheartedly. Emily's father secretly smiled at the ethical behavior Luigi had shown in their small house even though Delfin knew Luigi's color and lifestyle, which were far from his usual Italian life.

Delfin was shocked at the foreigner's behavior. He just secretly smiled though they didn't have a pleasant first encounter.

Until came the next sunrise, Delfin did not expect Luigi would insist on coming with him to the field to plant rice. The older man didn't want the visitor to do that, but he couldn't do anything. Luigi even took the lead, and Michael quickly followed after them.

In those moments, Delfin was holding the rope of his carabao. He couldn't do anything when the child insisted on going with them. Therefore, he called the child and quickly rode behind his carabao. Delfin made sure that the carabao was clean, and there was no mud in its body. The smile of the child could not fit on his lips.

The father could see how Michael was so fond of the carabao ride even though he had doubts about riding it at first until he lost his fear. Luigi's big smile also rested on his lips.

Delfin helped Michael to get off the carabao. They would then just walk on the embankments adjoining the stream and the field. Luigi noticed that the stream was bright and clean. Later on, they had to put their things in the cottage. Only palm and nipa huts serve as its roof.

Delfin quickly went down to the spot to continue with the rest of the crops. Luigi didn't know how to do it and how to get started.

Chapter Ten

Delfin noticed that, so he quickly approached Luigi and taught him what to do.

"This is how it is done. From a single crop, you will only take three or more roots of the paddy, and then you drop it into the pit. Afterwards, you measure a ledge, and again, you sink a bunch of the paddy."

Luigi quickly followed his instructions on how to plant rice until he realizes that he was capable and fast in planting, something he secretly enjoyed.

In those moments, Michael was just staring out of the hut. He would also like to step down, but Delfin restricted him.

Until the heat of the sun rose, and it was painful for the skin. However, Luigi did not mind the heat of the sun. He continued planting. The older man himself surrendered and told Luigi to get some shade under the hut first.

During those moments, Delfin glanced his shadow and estimated what time it was because the sun was so hot to the skin.

"Luigi, that's enough and go under the shade. Emily is already there. She has lunch for us," Delfin told Luigi.

Luigi quickly glanced at the oncoming girl before returning to planting. Michael's eyes overgrew, too. He got up and ran to Emily. In those moments, Emily began to walk faster. The lady quickly embraced the child, something Emily was pleased. Whereas, Luigi's strange smile on his lips seemed like he didn't mind his tiredness. He was happy though he was exhausted from stooping while planting. Emily quickly prepared the food for the three to eat. She served food for the child first before Delfin, and the last one was Luigi. Delfin noticed that Luigi has a secret glance for his daughter. It was not new to him because he had gone through such systems.

It would also be alright if Luigi's desire to get in the Philippines was to court Emily. The young man had the right way of dealing with the girl's parents. For him, even if it is already modern, the practice of courting by young men should still be old-fashioned because that's right.

They lived in the middle of the field and, at the same time, lived their old ways. Time had not changed their early culture. For Delfin, that's all he could be proud of to anyone, which he had inherited from his ancestors. So even some people were repurchasing his farm, he refused them for his farm would be converted into a subdivision.

It was enough for him to have burnt rice to make coffee with added brown sugar. In that way, he was happy.

Although it was said that there's a modern age, Delfin was still old-fashioned. That's what he wanted for his children to know, especially Emily. Goodness that Emily was not brainwashed from the modern age and new kinds of stuff today.

"Let's have a bath!" Michael asked his nanny to join him.

"Haa?!" Emily was surprised because she didn't expect that from the kid.

"Let's go!" Michael suddenly held Emily's hand, and she couldn't resist the boy's wish.

The two quickly went down without Michael removing his clothes. At those moments, Luigi just smiled at him and Emily.

"Why don't you try too, Luigi? The water in our place is fresh!" said Delfin.

"Haa?!"

Luigi quickly stood up and ran straight into the water. Emily was startled by that unexpected encounter.

"You went down too?!"

"The water here is clean and clear. Your place is well-taken care of!"

"There are many buyers in this vast land. Others want this to be a subdivision while they wanted in that area to be a factory. But my father did not agree!"

"Why?!"

"He is happy with the sceneries. He won't replace them with delicious foods that are almost chemically processed.

He does not want to train himself with nice equipment, and he does not want to go with the modern times. For him, it is his paradise.

So, until now, we can still eat rice that we have grown and cultivated. The fresh air also improves my father's health, away from the smoky exhaust of jeeps and factories, and fresh vegetables gathered around the house. This is what my father couldn't trade for so many good things around."

"That's why it's nice to live here with you. You are rich in everything!"

"You're right!"

"But what makes you come to Italy while you don't need anything more here?" Luigi asked.

"We were arguing about that with my father. I always disobeyed what he wanted. Let's say, and I just liked it because of the Vatican that I could just see on TV. It is my dream to see that and go to the cold side of the world like Rome. And besides, I want to visit the Lourdes in Paris. It's so lovely. There's a place like that here in Bulacan."

"But I'm so glad you came to Rome!"

"Why?"

"If that didn't happen, I probably wouldn't be here, and we wouldn't have met!"

Emily secretly smiled as to what the man told her. But she didn't do anything to make Luigi notice it. The three of them continued to bathe while Delfin was watching.

After that, they returned to the field to continue planting. In those moments, Luigi and Emily had touched each other's hands accidentally. Luigi held it tightly, but Emily quickly took away her hands from Luigi.

"Sorry!"

Emily did not respond to Luigi's words anymore. But she smiled a bit that made Luigi happy.

"You know, I already saw the girl who was going to be the mother of my son, Michael," Luigi said.

"Ha? Really? Where is she?"

"I'm in front of her."

"You!"

Emily blushed. She didn't expect to hear it from the mouth of her boss. So, she quickly got out of the water, but Luigi was quick to respond. He promptly grabbed Emily's hand to stop her. At that moment, Emily's father was coming back on the field.

"I'll prove to you how much I love you!" Luigi said to her.

Emily ignored Luigi's words. She quickly went up and headed the hut. There, Emily packed their things. When she was done packing, she immediately signaled the kid as they went back to the house.

Luigi knew he had a lot to do with his love for Emily. He just continued his courtship. Although he knew for himself that he was not accustomed to all that Emily's father did, such as cutting the woods, fetching watering from the well, even cleaning the pig cage, he still did them.

Emily, in turn, was also falling in love with her boss. She was sure of it. She couldn't control her feelings anymore.

Even climbing the coconut tree, Luigi made it. Unfortunately, when he was in the middle of a tree branch, he suddenly slipped and continued to fell down the ground. Luigi tried to bring out his beautiful smile, but he couldn't do it because of the severity of his fall and the scar he had on his arms. Emily quickly approached him.

"Are you okay?"

"I'm fine."

Luigi's heart was pounding at Emily's concern. However, Emily didn't make him notice even though she knew her heart was beating so hard. Luigi saw it all, something he pleased. He noticed that Emily was secretly loving him, too.

Emily personally took care of her visitor to treat his arm injuries. His skin was almost peeled off. Luigi could feel the pain of his wounds, but he did not want the lady to notice it. He only smiled at Emily while he was being treated, even though he had difficulty hiding the pain in his arm.

It was Emily who took him to the river to catch fish. Both felt that they're happy in all their ways. Here, they became closer together.

"Until now, I don't even know what my state in your heart is," Luigi joked.

"It's not easy to accept your love," said Emily.

"Why? Is it hard to love me?"

"Until now, I do not know what's your position in the life of your spouse. She still doesn't want me to be at peace!" revealed Emily to Luigi.

"I've finished everything between the two of us. I'm just waiting for the court's decision!"

"But!"

Luigi suddenly embraced Emily and quickly kissed the girl on her lips. Emily couldn't resist. Her body was resisting but not her heart, something that made it difficult for her to decide. But her love for Luigi prevailed, and she just let him drown in his love.

Emily let Luigi decide what he wanted. She could no longer disagree with all his plans. She just backed off when…

"I love you, too, Luigi!" Emily suddenly uttered.

She then had given her love to the man who had just made her life happier. It was not until the darkness reached them that they decided to go home. The fear settled in Emily's heart. How could she explain to his father on coming back

late at night while she just said that they would just go out for a while?

However, Emily and Luigi's beautiful smiles were indescribable. She convinced herself that she needed to reciprocate the love promised to her by the man she had just loved and to add, a foreigner.

Inside the house, Emily quickly got her father's hand to do the Filipino practice of respecting elders or "pagmamano". This is a custom that was not removed from the culture they carried until they grew up. But she could still feel frightened from Delfin, as she spent the night with Luigi. However, she remained to be calm in front of his father.

"Why are you so late?!" asked Delfin.

"We had a wonderful time strolling around. Sorry, we're late!" Luigi quickly answered.

Emily did not speak anymore when she noticed that the father was already satisfied with Luigi's response.

"Get your dinner ready, my daughter, and maybe our guest is hungry!"

Emily quickly obeyed her father's command. Some days passed by, and it was noteworthy that the two were happy. Emily had already shown her love for Luigi, and Delfin noticed it. Emily's father always glanced at the two. Emily also became more affectionate to Michael, the son of her love. She did not expect herself to fall in love with Michael's father and then be his girlfriend that further deepened their relationship.

"She loved Luigi even before!" Delfin said to himself. "She made sure of it to herself, and that was what made her happy."

At that moment, Michael was smiling at her actions.

"Are you happy?" asked Michael to the lady.

"Ha?" Then she hugged the child.

"Yes, I'm happy! The happiest!"

She, even more, tightened her embrace to the child.

"Oh, I'm trapped!"

"Sorry, sorry. Hehehe!"

Until she laid in bed, she carried with her the love that seemed like she was in heaven.

"It's good to have someone you love!" said Emily to herself. In those moments, she didn't realize Michael was in front of her. Though he was still a child, he knew those smiles on her lips meant something, which made him happy. Even though he didn't see the reason behind those smiles, he was glad because he could see Emily, her nanny, happy.

"You, you are still looking at me!" said Emily to the boy as she caressed him. He tickled Michael to both his waists.

"It!" the boy happily mentioned to her. In those moments, Delfin just stared at her. She quickly regained her beautiful smile when her father noticed her.

Luigi smiled back as he glared at Emily while playing with Michael. The glances of the two brightened their sweet romance.

They were inside a mall in Pampanga when they didn't expect to see her best friend, Rosanna. Rosanna was her classmate when she was in elementary school.

"Emily!" shouted by the high-pitched voice of a person. Emily was sure she was being called, so she quickly turned around despite her doubts. She even followed herself with the desire to recognize the familiar voice of a young woman.

"Yes?" said Emily to the person calling her.

"You are!" said Rosanna.

"It's you, Rosanna!"

"I knew it! I can't be wrong. Look at how those fingers of yours move, and they are like Doña Buding's!"

"Oh, you! Until this day, you still have not changed. You are still joking! How are you? Well, you still know me!"

"How can I not recognize you as the only one I know in the whole world who has a shaky finger! You are beautiful, what's the secret?" asked Rosanna at the same time, looked at Emily's foreign companion, Luigi. Emily noticed that Rosanna's neck was almost twisted around her. She didn't want others to see her even though she began to be upset. She had just been forced to introduce Luigi to Rosanna. She didn't want to introduce him to her because she knew her classmate as a man-getting, exceptionally if handsome. She would do everything even to quarrel with her friend.

But in those moments, Emily became calm.

He thought Luigi would not let their relationship destroy just because Rosanna suddenly entered their lives.

Emily was jealous of her friend, Rosanna. She knew that Rosanna would not miss the man who had captured Emily's heart. Emily made herself look casual so she wouldn't look like a villain in front of her boyfriend, Luigi.

"He is Luigi, my boss," Emily told friend Rosanna.

"She is my girlfriend!" said Luigi.

Even though Emily was surprised, she was happy. She felt like angels in heaven lullabied her. She felt like her feet were stepping in the air.

Chapter Eleven

I n frustration, Emily's smile widened, and Rosanna noticed it. It was enough for her to know where she was in Luigi's heart.

"Your boyfriend is kind. He doesn't want you to call her the boss," Rosanna said. Emily was envious of Rosanna's personality.

Luigi himself had told his girlfriend to leave. Rosanna became even more envious of her friend's condition. She waited for the two lovers to almost disappear before turning her gaze to others.

"I hope to see you again one day, alone.

I'll make sure you will never lose my warm kisses!" said Rosanna to herself with a threat.

It was noteworthy that her smile was different for the man she had just met. She smiled to herself as she remembered how she had pressed Luigi's palm as they held hands. Rosanna held Luigi's hand with a teasing smile. At that moment, Luigi suddenly became agitated at the behavior of Emily's friend. But he didn't make Emily notice it as he

looked at the girl he had just faced. Luigi just secretly smiled at the behavior of Emily's friend.

"Hehehe! Naughty!" Michael's father had just shrugged himself.

Luigi would have liked to look back at Rosanna, but Emily could see and start a fight. He knew for himself that he would never replace Emily with any other woman.

For him, he had enough hard work for this woman to get. So, he would never make an excuse just to fight. That's what Luigi had in mind.

It was early morning when they were halfway down the "highway" to Manila to fix the missing passports and some essential documents needed for the family to return to Rome. Emily would be there shortly after Luigi and Laura's divorce ends. This was also what Luigi's longing for.

It was late in the afternoon when they were finished with their purpose. It was because of the long queue and being busy inside the embassy. It was Luigi who decided to visit the Mall of Asia near the embassy. Luigi was surprised at the size and width of the mall in Manila. But all that he just shrugged. What matters to him was to be with the woman who really had his heartbeat and loved his son Michael very much.

It was not difficult to bring the child closer to her because she raised him.

So that was one of the reasons Luigi was forced to go to the Philippines when his son came in search of the woman, he considered the second mother. But in his own heart, it was his heart that commanded him to find the woman who made his heartbeat and opened again to love. It was just a bonus that his son asked to find and return to Rome his Yaya Emily.

At the airport in Manila, Emily broke down in tears as she had brought Luigi and Michael, something heavy on her heart.

It was difficult for her because it took almost two months for the family to leave the Philippines. It seemed to be hard for Emily to lose Luigi and Michael in her life suddenly. She wanted to stop the two, but she couldn't help but cry and couldn't stop it. Luigi and Michael noticed it all.

"I'll be back with Michael," Luigi told Emily. Michael hugged his nanny immediately when he heard what his father had said.

Emily wanted to go to Italy again. She thought they wanted to come back and take her to Italy, so they went to the Philippines.

That's because of Michael. But it was hard for Emily to return because of what happened to her in Rome, which Michael's mother, Laura, did. However, her decision to return someday to the place he had longed for and loved, Rome, was already finalized.

She had not thought that in Rome, she would find her love that would give her life and meaning in her character, even though it was the cause of her bad experience. This was when she was jailed there and alleged as the kidnapper. But all of that had not been proven because of the defense testimony made by Michael.

Emily's father, Delfin, did not like her plans to return to Italy.

"You're not coming back to Europe, Emily!"

"But I do feel sorry for the boy. The boy was adamant that I should go back to Italy again!"

"Is it the kid or your boss, Luigi?!"

"I love Luigi."

"I think the reason behind your imprisonment is because his wife thought you were Luigi's mistress!" Delfin said angrily.

"Luigi and I have never had a relationship! Only now that I answered and received his love."

"You will not be leaving for Europe just to be a house helper again!" Delfin said, then he turned his back and left his daughter in the kitchen.

By that time, Emily's family was having dinner. Emily thought about her father's decision. She thought that it was the end for her and Luigi. It was madness to go back to Italy just for the love she had for Luigi. The love she gave for the child who she raised was also difficult for her to forget.

For Emily, you could ask anything to her but not to be far away from the man who made her heart beating. It was until she broke down in tears, and Emily was helpless to defend herself for the right to love. That's what his mother, Adang, noticed.

"You are looking that far. Is Michael the reason?" Emily's mother said to her. Emily nodded. "But that's not enough for me to believe you that he is the only reason."

"Why is that so? I fall in-loved only once, but it seems wrong."

Emily watched the sunset. As she watched, her mother noticed her tying the carabao with a rope around a tree.

"Is it wrong to love a man like Luigi?" Emily asked her to approach mother.

"It's never a mistake to love!" said Adang to her daughter.

"But why didn't Dad like Luigi? He is kind!"

"Luigi is not the problem here, but what happened to you in Rome. You are incarcerated because you have been charged with kidnapping Michael. It hurts us that we couldn't even help you in the time you were in trouble!"

In those moments, Emily was just looking at her mother, with the sunset in which its light was the only light from their home's window.

"Your father is so worried about you!" said Adang. Emily just kept looking at her mom.

"I saw how worried he was. He couldn't help but cry out in the vast darkness. His eyes were swollen because he was thirsty for your hugs and affection.

He can't get rid of it because you are our first daughter who gave us joy here in our little house," said Adang to her daughter Emily.

Emily continued to watch the setting of the moon. Meanwhile, Adang continued her work.

Emily just cried as a response to her questions to herself. Many things troubled her mind.

Delfin got up early to milk the carabao. He used to bring the milk to his regular customer, Nora, to make it white cheese. According to Nora, it is the favorite delicacy of people who are socially and politically prominent. In those moments, Emily went and stopped in front of her father. Delfin just ignored and kept on what he was doing.

"Dad, sorry!" cried Emily at the same time, hugging her dad even though he was busy doing something.

Delfin stood up and confronted his daughter, Emily.

"For what?" asked her father.

"From understanding to all that I have not done well."

"You know, I feel ashamed to myself for everything. I never saw you become so strong after all. When you were imprisoned in Rome, my heart was in fear because you were far from me. I told myself why I allowed you to go there. I couldn't do anything. I just looked up to heaven and prayed for your safety and freedom. It seemed to me like my life before when the family of your mother thought of accepting me." Delfin's world stopped temporarily and looked around.

"If you look at the extent of our surroundings, that is what your mother's family-owned before we had a relationship. I have suffered many hardships in the field of trial. This vast land has caused us to destroy our love and trust in each other of not letting go. Your mother fought for me to her father that the luxury of life was not a reason for me to love Adang. Your mother's family thought that I was after their livelihood, and love was not the reason." Suddenly, Delfin glanced at the surroundings and looked at the places his eyes could gaze.

"That's why your grandparents didn't want me when I was courting then. I made your mother feel the purity of my love and not what she had, even though she was blind.

I made her feel that she was the only gift God had given me. Eventually, your grandparents welcomed me when I made this land, where we live, wealthier."

Delfin looked back at her daughter, Emily.

"Now, if you succeed in Rome, you have long dreamed of coming back, even if at first your dream has crumbled, go ahead and carry on. Maybe this is what God has given you, and Luigi is your love."

Emily was shocked when she heard it from her father. She didn't expect that from Delfin. She was at last free to return to Rome, Italy.

"Yes, thank you, Father!" said Emily embracing her father.

"I made a mistake that you have your own life and that you have to decide. When you fall again, get up and continue the fight. Just fight, my child.

You must fight for whatever you go through." said Delfin embracing his daughter.

"Thanks, Dad!"

"In Rome, whatever you face in the challenge of life, you fight.

Ultimately, you are the winner. Just don't let the enemy beat you. I know you are a fighter, my child!" repeatedly uttered by her father.

"Thank you very much, Dad!"

Delfin gave her daughter a tight hug. He was confident to know that her daughter would follow her boyfriend and Michael, that he didn't want before.

In those moments, Emily wept with joy as she was about to see Michael and Luigi. That's all she had in mind.

Inside the airport, Emily's feet are restless as she walks down the broad aisle in anticipation of seeing who she treated as her family members, Luigi and Michael.

Her mind was far from the threat she could face in Europe. All she could think about was to get to the land of her dreams.

Inside the plane, she couldn't even sleep during the long trip. Emily was just pondering and cherishing the good memories she had in Rome when she also suddenly realized that her fight against her boss, Laura, was not yet over.

"I wish I could just avoid her by the time I get to Rome and try to prevent her from meeting again!"

She was at the airport in Rome (Flumicino) when Luigi and Michael were already in the lobby. Luigi gave a hug and a warm kiss to his girl-friend, Emily. Even though Emily was a little lost, she kissed him back, too. After that, she quickly embraced Michael, who she raised. She could hardly explain the child's excitement as if her real mother was here. Maybe that's what the kid was thinking of her as he almost jumped in to hug Emily. It also took a long time before she let go of holding the kid. She never loathed his tight embrace.

They stopped at a restaurant to eat before heading to their flat where they were staying.

Even though Emily was nervous, she never made them notice that she wanted to act normally like before. But Luigi and Michael noticed it. However, she casually answered their questions to her until she calmed down.

Inside the condominium, Emily was hesitant to step inside, even though she trusted her peers like Luigi and his son Michael. She was fully convinced that she would stay in Michael's room, but Luigi made sense of her first.

"Here is our room. We have our place to sleep," Luigi said.

"Haa?!" asked Emily while wondering.

"Don't you want me to sleep with you?" Luigi asked with a smile on his lips.

Suddenly, Emily coughed as if she was drowning without drinking water. But she made everything normal.

It was already late at night, and Michael already slept the happiness he was not expecting when his tata arrived. It was then the first time that Emily and Luigi will be sleeping in one bed. Emily had never experienced in all her life that there was a man beside her in bed.

She quickly went into the bathroom, which was also inside the bedroom, while Luigi was waiting for her in bed.

When Emily decided to get out of the bathroom, she saw Luigi waiting for her. Though nervous, she made herself casual so that Luigi couldn't notice it.

Emily was startled from sitting on the edge of the bed. Luigi suddenly stood up.

Luigi slowly approached the girl, something she did not expect. She was kissed on the lips with her mouth still closed, obviously inexperienced at such events. Luigi felt the girl's strong heartbeat.

He noticed that Emily didn't expect what she was going to experience that night. But Luigi planned to end her fears. All he wanted was to make sure he had that night and that he had Emily.

He repeated to try opening Emily's mouth with his mouth. She tried to squeeze even a small part of her mouth to allow his hot kisses to enter. But Emily only closed her mouth. Luigi was looking for a way to lit up the fresh wood that was long-held by each touch of his lips. Luigi took a different approach. He went down around her neck. Again, he lit her lips and warmed the moist wood.

Luigi was unconscious when suddenly, the girl's hands clasped his neck. He could feel the warmth of each girl's revenge on him. He also felt Emily's new move even he compensated for the warmth of his lips.

Here, Luigi was delighted that his future wife had no experience. Luigi changed his move. He had lowered his lips to Emily's breast. In those moments, the girl became stranded. Emily didn't expect such a kiss. She just secretly enjoyed it.

"Oh, that's the kiss!" said Emily to herself.

Emily was happy with what Luigi had done to her. Suddenly, there was a knock on the door that they were not expecting. They knew Michael was sleeping in his room. They quickly opened the door. They were just surprised when Michael was at the door.

"Why are you still awake?" Luigi asked the son.

"I'm alone in my room. I'll just be sleeping next to you!" said Michael to two. Luigi and Emily just looked at each other. The girl laughed secretly.

In those moments, the two couldn't do anything. Michael quickly entered the room. He reached over to the bed and lay down between them. The two looked deeper, something

that pleased Emily with Michael's behavior. The two of them had just slept with their unfinished romance. Emily noticed that Luigi's mood had changed, caused by Michael's behavior. He could do nothing with his behavior.

In a regular job, Emily personally brings the school to Michael. At two o'clock in the afternoon, she was fetching the kid again. Emily was tireless in her daily routine. Luigi had high trust in Emily because she loved the child.

Luigi returned to Germany for his work there. He traveled to Rome weekly for vacation. He was happy because he knew that Emily would never leave her son Michael.

"I have no mistake in loving her compared to Laura. She loved nothing but herself!" said Luigi to himself. Luigi just sighed. What he had in mind was that he was caring for her son Michael and even Emily.

Luigi was just continuing his work on the site. But he could not help but look forward to returning to Rome for his two loved ones.

Chapter Twelve

Emily got busy caring for Michael. After leaving school, they hurried down so Michael can play in the park. It was the child's usual way when with Emily. While there was a chance, Emily would talk with nannies like her in the park. She still used to look after Michael often even when she was talking to her friend, Rona, who was from Bulacan and had been in Rome for a long time.

Rona also had an Italian boyfriend and was about the same age as Luigi. So, it was not difficult for them to talk about their loved one's behavior. It was noteworthy, however, that Emily did not want to talk about her boyfriend, Luigi, especially with her countrymen and fellow women.

For her, the issue when it comes to love was sacred and private. She didn't want to practice herself in informing the whole world about their relationship. She thought that they were not even celebrities to showcase their relationship. It was just that she knew Luigi loved her, and that was enough.

It was during those moments that she suddenly remembered Laura, who became a disturbance in her mind. And then unexpectedly, Laura came.

Emily was unaware of Laura's arrival because the latter passed in the backyard. She was surprised and started to think.

"Oh? Are you stuck? You look like a ghost!" said Laura.

Emily was surprised by the unexpected change in Laura's attitude.

"Haa?!"

Laura was the one who approached Emily for a hug and a kiss on the cheek, something Emily didn't expect. However, she just became calm.

Emily still showed respect even she had worries in her heart and mind. Nevertheless, she was ready for whatever Laura had planned for her.

"You have to disappear from my son's path, Emily!" Laura said angrily to herself. She quickly changed her look so that her son Michael and Emily could not figure out her evil plan for her son's nanny.

Emily's smile was compounded by what Laura had shown her. She knew for herself that Laura had something terrible to do with her. She knew that Laura had treated her with contempt.

"I need to be prepared for what she plans on me!" said Emily to herself.

It was during those moments that Laura gazed sharply at Emily. "Get ready, Emily! You have to get lost in the path of my son as his nanny. Because I don't want you to be my child's second mother, that's not going to happen, hmp!" Laura said angrily to herself. Laura made mean smiles.

One Saturday, Luigi was expected to arrive, and they would bond with his son, Michael.

That's what the boy had been waiting for since his father promised him about it. So, Emily also expected that she would be with them.

While they were inside the mall, the child's happiness was very unusual. He held both hands of the two persons that made him happy, which then noticed by his father. Emily secretly smiled at Michael's behavior.

The three watched the movie, Dumbo. The theme of the film was for kids, that's why the two could traced happiness from the child's face knowing that smile was hard to find for kids like Michael.

After that, they entered an expensive restaurant that Luigi used to visit. Although Emily was unfamiliar with such a kind, she assured herself that she would not disappoint Luigi and Michael.

Since she was unable to get used to that kind of life, Luigi quickly grabbed the lady's hand. Luigi felt Emily's skepticism. Emily promptly looked at her boyfriend.

"Well, well, well!" said Laura.

They did not expect Laura to enter the same restaurant.

"Laura, don't do scandal here. This is not the right place!" said Luigi.

"Luigi, this is a classy place. I'm a celebrity, and I'm not going to lower my level like what you're thinking!"

Laura quickly kissed Michael. After that, she also left with the famous movie director. Luigi just looked at the two away.

In those moments, Emily was startled by Laura's unexpected appearance. Michael just looked at his mother. The boy's respect was still there. He paid respect to her after his mother approached him.

It was late at night when the three returned to the condo. Michael had taken advantage of the opportunity. He quickly went to his father's room. Emily and Luigi just looked at each other because they could do nothing but follow the child to the bedroom.

As usual, Michael was in the middle. Luigi and Emily were on both sides. Later, they noticed that the child was tired. Luigi quickly figured his way out.

"Let's go to the floor!" Luigi told Emily.

She just looked at Luigi. Emily shook her head and indicated that she didn't want it to happen.

The girl could hear the eyes of his boyfriend, but Emily was very firm and didn't like what Luigi wanted.

Until then, they had slept their desire to make love on the floor. Emily secretly smiled at Luigi's childlike behavior of not granting his wish. Luigi just crouched in the corner until he fell asleep. As a result, Emily laughed to herself.

Laura, along with her boyfriend Mauro, were always arguing about her husband and her son, Michael. Laura wanted to get her son from Luigi, but Mauro didn't agree. But in the end, he approved. Michael was with Laura on weekends. During school days, Luigi had the kid.

Mauro was a model, much more appealing than Umberto. His stance was similar to Hollywood's celebrity.

Laura was eager to see her son, Michael. Luigi also agreed to have Michael with Laura on weekends. On the other hand, he was with him during the school days. Though Laura was with a helper and had done the same before, she was still rattling.

Laura was almost at the door and waiting for someone to do the doorbell. She was waiting for her son to arrive. She used to go and look the clock back on the wall of her house. At that moment, Mauro could only look at her actions. But Mauro entered the room.

He didn't have the patience to wait for Laura's son. Shortly after that, there was a doorbell, something that she was expecting.

Laura opened the door personally. And as she expected, Michael was at the door with her nanny Emily. Laura did not let Michael notice that she wanted to change her face in front of Emily. But Laura didn't want herself to start the tension. She wanted peace to begin with her. At that time, she had enough to see her son, Michael.

Laura didn't spend much time on the person who deprived the love of her son and her husband.

Laura knew for herself that Mauro had been in her life, and she loved him.

Michael enjoyed his mom's warm welcome to his nanny. That's what he should expect, accepting the fact that their worlds are different. Even as a child, Michael already knew what his parent's situation was. He had been trying to understand this since he was young.

Michael and Emily were in the living room. Laura just let the kid play there as she continued to sip her hot tea. Suddenly, Mauro came out of the room. Laura did not expect him to go out of the room, wearing only his brief and no upper clothes.

Emily was shocked by what she saw, but she didn't let them notice it. Emily didn't like what she saw.

She just tried to be calm. Until it was late afternoon, and it was time for Emily and Michael to leave Laura's house.

Emily relaxed as she stepped out of the building where Laura was living. If she would only be followed, she would not be there the next time the child goes on vacation. That's what her mind was screaming. But she couldn't do anything because it was included with her promise to her boyfriend, Luigi, to watch over Michael, especially when he's in Laura's place.

Emily just shrugged at herself because she didn't just want to see Laura but Mauro, especially in the way how he showed up in the house.

"Rude, hmp!" said Emily to herself.

At Michael's mother's condo, Laura and Mauro argued over what he did when his son's nanny was there.

"Why do you pay so much attention to what I did when I came out of our room wearing only a brief? I'm in this house!" said Mauro to Laura.

"Please, once they come back next time, get dressed and be decent in everything you do!" said Laura.

Laura suddenly left when she finished saying what she wanted to tell her boyfriend Mauro, who then proceeded to their room.

But in those moments, Mauro had secret smiles because he couldn't help but fell in love with Emily's beautiful face.

Any man could easily be trapped in Emily's heart. That was Mauro's view, so he couldn't wonder Laura was so upset at her son's nanny and has been replaced by her ex-husband.

"I will let you love me, Emily!" said Mauro to himself.

Mauro noticed that his girlfriend was no longer angry with her son's nanny.

But he knew she was jealous when she didn't like Mauro wearing a brief only even though he used to do it before.

She was very jealous now every time she was in front of Emily, and when they were talking about her, something that makes Mauro think.

"Her beauty is so different. She has a strong appearance, and that was hard to forget about her. How can I get closer to her?!" said Mauro to himself. Mauro secretly smiled to himself. He couldn't explain the thrill in his heart.

"I will crush your scent in my arms. You will love me to the end!" Mauro told himself with threatening. It smiled again as if it were easy to get Emily. That's what Mauro had in mind.

"I'm going to crush your scent, hehehe!"

It was during those moments that Laura watched him in his strange gestures, something that had changed him from Mauro's former practice. Laura had some thoughts.

"Hmmm, something is playing in your mind, Mauro. I need to know what you are thinking! If Emily is the reason for your smiles, you should never dream of making her in love with you.

You will not succeed because someone already owns Emily's heart, and that is my ex-husband, Luigi. So, you are wasting your time paying attention to her."

Again, he watched Mauro's actions.

"You're just going to fail, Mauro, because you are mine!"

But the opportunity seemed tempting. During those times, Laura was not in the mood to be jealous of her boyfriend Mauro. She assured herself that Mauro loved her and would never betray her even when sometimes she got jealous. Mauro worked as a model for a branded garment.

There would be a model program to be held in Paris, France. This was one of the hottest programs when it comes to elegant clothes, and Laura would participate in it. She forced herself to think that Mauro would do nothing wrong, especially he and Emily would be left to the child, something that made her feel more nervous. Laura would be gone for more than a week without Mauro.

There was a large van for her personal belongings to use in Paris, France. While she used her car, a white Ferrari, that she drove herself, and made the vehicle dashed to the airport.

All of her staff just looked as they brought her belongings. After arriving at the airport, she just closed the car's door quickly and left the car in the parking lot.

Her secretary was waiting for her to fix her airport queue and luggage. After passing through the detector machine, she promptly got her personal belongings, which also passed through a similar device for proper inspection of things to avoid hustle in the flight. She then quickly picked up her things.

She was in the first-class section of the plane and was almost seated beside the pilot. Here, she quickly leaned her chair and lied as if it were a single bed, with the help of the plane's crew.

Some people wanted to approach her, but she was guarded tightly that no could easily approach her. Because she's a model and an actress, it's not easy for anyone to get to know her personally. Laura just enjoyed herself in listening to music and closed her eyes. Even though she was wearing sunglasses, it was reflective that her eyes were already shut, something she didn't realize that people were looking at her, even the pilot.

At the airport in Paris, there were assigned people that were ready to welcome her. Even the limousine car that she would be using was also set. Laura would just ride.

The car quickly left having Laura in it. Until she arrived at the lobby of the hotel that she would be staying. Laura was taken aback at the height of the hotel, but she didn't let others notice her amusement.

She proceeded to the elevator as she knew that another secretary was waiting for her at that hotel.

As she entered her room, she quickly opened her cellphone. She immediately began the video where she could watch whatever was going on at home. That's what Mauro didn't know. Laura took advantage of the opportunity to have CCTV screened in her home so that she could see all of his moves, by the time Emily was there.

This was also to ensure that Mauro would not do anything wrong if it were indeed true executing his evil intentions.

After trying to figure out everything she had put in place, she just let it be opened for her to know what was going on. She left the cellphone first and went to the bathroom to look at herself in the mirror.

It was at those moments that Mauro opened the door, then a paid woman appeared before the door and entered the house. At about that same time, Laura quickly went out of the bathroom. However, she failed to watch the video that had been turned on.

She didn't even enable the save setting of the video. She was unaware that Mauro was not doing good, that he also got a paid woman from the street.

Mauro didn't know what Laura did to bait him. However, Mauro was careful about what he did. He also carefully looked around to make sure there would be no disagreements between him and Laura by the time she returned from work. To make sure, he let the paid woman left through the window, and Laura would have no clues when she would arrive. During those moments, Laura forgot to record the video. It was too late when she saw that it had not been saved.

Laura had no idea that Mauro had come up with a way to avoid getting caught.

Mauro personally took care of Laura's son to stay with him, something neither Emily nor Michael expected. In those moments, Emily was not in the mood.

She noticed something was wrong with Mauro's behavior. Mauro did nothing but glanced at her, but Emily just ignored him. She thought to be careful and not go too far from Michael so that Mauro would not have the chance if he had any plans.

Chapter Thirteen

Emily nearly pulled out a thorn in the chest when it was getting dark. That's all she had to wait for her to get out of Laura's house right away. Her speed was just as fast as the lightning so she could go far.

As they arrived at Luigi's condo, Emily quickly locked the door. She made sure the door was closed correctly, and she temporarily left the child in the living room. After that, she quickly went to the bathroom to bathe. At that moment, Michael suddenly knocked on the door.

"Ci?" asked Emily, who was still in the bathroom.

"It's Daddy!" said Michael.

Emily quickly dressed and went out so she could immediately answer Luigi's call from Germany.

"Ci?" said Emily.

"How are you?" asked Luigi on the other line.

"I'm okay right now. How about you?"

"I miss you, and I love you!"

"Me, too. Take care!"

The phone conversation had ended. Then, Michael suddenly called from the living room while watching cartoons on the television

"When is Daddy coming home? I'm missing him."

"On Saturday night, Daddy's here!"

"Did you miss Daddy?" Michael teased his nanny. Emily just nodded and smiled at Michael's question.

In those moments, Michael just continued watching the television. Emily prepared a meal for him while he was in front of the television. And as Emily watched the boy, he thought Michael was happy to be alone with her in the condo.

The night was profound. Michael was already accustomed to sleeping in the middle of watching the television. So, she quickly took the child and set him in his room near the master's bedroom. That's also where Emily stayed, which she always did when they were just two. Michael, on the other hand, was glad that Emily was always beside him in bed.

Laura had always envied Emily because Emily is closer than to Michael than his mother. This was what Laura and Luigi always argued about until Laura got used to their fight. Laura was no longer with Luigi and Michael. She had her own life and new love in Mauro's image. He was whom Laura poured herself so hard.

If she used to bring Michael to Laura's house, it was because she also felt sad when the child was not with her. On the other hand, Mauro didn't feel any closeness to the boy because, in the first place, he was not his child. But Laura loved Mauro so much that she couldn't leave the man for she thought he loved her, and he kept on following all of Laura's desire. Unlike Luigi, she couldn't control his character.

Mauro was obedient to everything she wanted. The only thing she could not get out of Mauro's personality was their frequent quarrel as he was always associated with the women he met on almost every occasion.

Laura looked at her wristwatch. It was late at night, but their program was not yet finished. Headache wrapped her heart as she thought of her boyfriend, Mauro, being left in their condo. But she made herself calm because it was her turn to step outside the stage. She was tired, but she just ignored it. What also puzzled her was the condition of her son, Michael, in her condo with his nanny, Emily. She knew for herself that Emily was Mauro's target and that he had a plan to make her love him. That was what she couldn't accept herself. "Emily already got Luigi and Michael from me. It can't be Mauro also." That's what Laura had in mind.

After a memorable moment in her work as a fashion model, Laura quickly returned to Rome because she longed for her fiancé Mauro. She decided to buy some pieces of clothing that she would give to her boyfriend that she carried and did not ask help from her assistant.

Laura had her key. She inserted the key into the door's keyhole, turned, and pushed the white door to open. She continued walking until she reached the master's bedroom. She was expecting Mauro was in the room waiting for her arrival. She slowly opened the door to surprise her boyfriend, who she thought was asleep and didn't notice her arrival.

She caught Mauro lying on his chest. On the other side of Mauro's cheek, Laura kissed him, and he was surprised. This caused the young man to wake up. Laura didn't expect him to wake up, so she quickly showed some pieces of the paper bag containing expensive personal items for Mauro. The big man's smile came out. Laura noticed that he was happy that she came and so, she was happy, too.

Mauro quickly grabbed Laura's hand and lost her balance. She fell unintentionally into the empty bed. The young man kissed Laura quickly. Laura did not expect this, but she did not resist the warm kisses of the young man until they slowly removed their clothes. They both tasted the sweetness of the moment.

Even though Laura was tired, she was happy how Mauro welcomed her. She felt like he was looking forward to seeing her after a few days of working away from him. She was happy with every touch of Mauro in her smooth skin. In those moments, Mauro was happy with what he was doing to Laura, even though it was against his feelings. However, Mauro heated Laura some more, which she enjoyed and drowned in happiness. It was like repayment for what Mauro had done in betraying her.

Until they were both tired in those moments, Mauro quickly covered up themselves with a blanket as Laura didn't care that she had just slipped out of bed after making each other happy.

It was until they fell asleep naked like Eve and Adam. Still, Laura felt eternal happiness.

Luigi had just returned from his work in Germany. A big smile could be seen on Michael's lips. While Emily's smile hide in the corner, she could not explain her happiness. Emily was happy when Michael's dad was there. Even though their relationship was formal, she still had this queer feeling. She knew for herself that she was still a young lady and that she had never dared to break her honor even to Luigi. Like what they used to do, Luigi requested them to go to an expensive restaurant for dinner.

So, Emily didn't prepare their food anymore, as Luigi told her while he was on the trip. Emily just made herself ready, along with Michael, who had long been anticipating his father's arrival. The three were happy until the evening was over. Luigi noticed that the child was already feeling restless and wasn't made to wait to return to the condo where they were staying. They were already in the garage when Luigi opened the door of the car on the other side before he opened the door near Emily. It was Luigi who carried Michael going inside the condo where they were staying. Until they got into Michael's room and there, they left the boy asleep.

They slowly got out of the kid's room, and the two went to the master's bedroom. Emily was speechless, but all of a sudden, she was surprised when Luigi held her shoulder. She assured herself that she was ready for any fight they would have that night. For the first time, Emily's chest sounded like a drum.

She could not be sure that there was a moment in herself that she would surely surrender to the man she loved most — her honor in exchange for eternal love. She would give it to the man who once made her happy and gave the meaning of love. Emily was speechless as Luigi slowly removed her upper dress.

But she quickly covered her chest with her arms. But Luigi removed it, and there, he started to kiss it intensely.

At that moment, Emily had a romantic excitement about what Luigi had done to her. She noticed that she didn't object to everything Luigi wanted to do. Later, she prepared herself and waited for Luigi's bold lips. But Emily only smiled at him. She was happy that Luigi came first to own her because she dreamed of giving herself only to the man she loved. It was a sign of her sincere love for him. It was at that moment that she appeared like Eve in the forest. Luigi glanced at Emily's entire face. Luigi noticed that Emily was still shy at him.

For the first time, he had seen the lady's whole. She quickly laid her down on the bed. Emily was surprised by what Luigi did. She felt Luigi's kiss came down from her chest down to Emily's waist until he wanted to go lower to her feminine part. Emily thwarted Luigi's plan to continue kissing her until at the very core of her personality. But Luigi quickly took Emily's hands. Emily couldn't help but noticed her strange joy as to what Luigi was making. She couldn't figure out why she didn't want to stop herself from holding back the fierce kisses the man was giving her. All she knew for herself was that she was ready to give whatever Luigi dreamed of owning her that night. She knew Luigi had long been waiting for her.

They seize the opportunity for the child to fall asleep so that they will not be disturbed in their precious moments of love and affection. Until Emily felt something strange happened to her.

She felt like there was something that was suddenly torn. Luigi was already expecting it. He knew he was the first man to enter the eternal heaven.

Emily wanted to cry, but she couldn't do it because she knew for herself that she was happy with what had happened to her that night. It was something she had just done for the man who she offered herself. Luigi also felt happy about that moment. Michael had not bothered the celebration of the two.

What matters was that both of them were happy and that they already knew for themselves that they were for each other. On the other hand, Laura didn't expect to have a job in Canada. She dreamed of being invited into the global field of clothing modeling. Little did Laura know that she was beautiful, tall, and strong in the appeal that everyone admired. She had long wanted to be invited to Canada. For her, it would be a great regret if she did not pursue it.

As usual, she entrusted the child to Mauro while she was away. Laura was in Canada for her meeting for the famous Loren Passion Product.

There was nothing to cheer Laura for the extra work that will lift her.

She faced a new challenge in the new world she lived in. Only a smile broke her lips as that was her exact dream she longed.

In those moments inside Laura's house, Emily was enjoying what she was doing. But she noticed that Mauro was following her, and changed his look. But Emily didn't let him notice because she didn't want it to start a fight.

Mauro even made a story to his girlfriend, Laura. Emily was careful when it came to what the ex-wife of her boss would say.

But she just figured that Mauro was following her because she refused to take her with Laura's car. So, it was only right for her to take the tram to the subway. With the crowd, the boy was almost trapped. However, Emily quickly protected him so that he could not be trapped by the sudden drop of passengers as they stopped at the terminal. She was about to go down when Emily was out of balance. She made a wrong step. That was why her foot went on the other side of the hole.

Emily got puzzled by what had happened to her. People screamed not to operate the tram. Her fears immediately swirled all over her that the train might run and break her leg. She was carefully removing her foot from the hole. Again, people shouted for the train not to operate so she could lift her leg. A few minutes passed, the lady's leg was finally removed from the hole.

Mauro was the one who encouraged Emily to step up and not to panic. Mauro noticed that her leg was severely scratched. When Emily's leg was removed from the hole, Mauro quickly carried her and rushed to the nearest hospital. In those moments, the crowd cheered over Mauro as he rescued the lady.

Eventually, the ambulance patrol arrived. Ambulance patrol assistants continued to care for the patient, Emily. In those moments, Mauro felt Emily squeezed his hand, something that made him smile. That was enough to get him closer to the lady. The child was left with Mauro, even though he didn't want to. But then, he had no choice.

That event provided a way for them to be in newspapers and television. At that moment, Luigi quickly watched it. It also didn't escape Laura's eyes.

Laura wanted to go home, but she could not leave her commitment to Canada. In those moments, she would be signing a contract. That was why she couldn't get rid of one of the most popular makeup and clothing products. Only famous people could buy then. But, Luigi quickly booked his flight to return to Rome immediately. He did not think that he might be sued for his job by making a sudden departure. What he needed to know was the condition of Emily and Michael from the accident. Luigi had just reached Rome in less than an hour from Germany. He quickly took taxing inline at Ciampino Airport. He told the driver of the hospital where he was going. Luigi's face was filled with a deep concern for his loved ones, Michael and Emily.

He was already in the hospital when Luigi saw a bad scene in the clinic. Mauro held Emily's hand, which made Luigi jealous. He still came close and unnoticed. In those moments, Michael was just around the corner. He was sitting alone and was still crying when he suddenly noticed Luigi.

"Daddy?!" he called his father.

There, Mauro slowly removed his hand from holding Emily's hand.

"How are you?" Luigi said to the lady.

In those moments, the girl just kept crying. She did not notice that in the corner of Luigi's smile was a seeming threat of jealousy. Emily was also being treated by the doctor, along with his assistant nurse.

Luigi looked deeply at the man who took Emily to the hospital. Mauro, on the other hand, was observing Luigi's actions. A few moments later, Emily could come home but needed a wheelchair to guide her from walking. Mauro lost his mind when they both almost held the end of the wheelchair handle. Luigi looked at Mauro until Mauro himself removed his hand from the handle.

Luigi personally pushed the wheelchair in which Michael was sitting with Emily. There was still sadness on Michael's face. Inside the condo where Luigi and his son live, Emily wanted to stand from the wheelchair to serve her boyfriend, who arrived from Germany. But Luigi quickly restrained Emily from continuing to stand.

"It's better for you to just rest," Michael said.

"We'll take care of you!" Emily just smiled at Luigi and Michael.

It was during those moments that she thought of Mauro, and she did not expect the suddenness of her admiration for the man she once hated. She could not understand herself. She never meant to think of Laura's boyfriend.

"He must just have been nice to me, and I didn't expect him to have a clean heart," Emily said to herself.

But all of that changed too quickly because he was just an illusion and she was unlikely to love a new man in her life. For her, Luigi was good enough. She had already given her honor, as well. She assured herself that she loved him and that she could never change her feelings.

For some days, Emily was not allowed to move around inside the condo. Luigi personally took care of bringing and fetching Michael to school while Emily was in bed. Luigi also used to bring food for Emily to eat at her bed, which made her happy because she had never experienced that all her life. She was happy and always had smiles on her lips.

She couldn't believe that her former employer was now the one serving her. She thought he loved her so much. That's why she was so happy for herself.

A few days passed until she was a month staying inside the condo. She decided to go to the kitchen to prepare something for her Luigi and Michael to eat. Although they didn't allow her to act, she forced herself.

Luigi had nothing to do when he saw the table all ready for their dinner. Michael quickly sat next to Emily while Luigi sat in his place. They were happily eating.

And when they had done eating, Emily was the one who stood up to clean the table. For her, the regular works in the house were not difficult at all, as the appliances were all electricals. Then, they quickly went to the living room, the favorite of the three to hangout. Emily and Luigi sat beside each other as they watched the child play alone. As usual, the child fell asleep when he got tired of playing. So, Michael's father quickly picked him up and put him into his room. But as he was removing his hand, he was surprised that Luigi was just hugged by the child, and he couldn't move. Emily just laughed. Luigi quickly signaled Emily to also sleep in the bed. The child would be just in the middle of them until all of them came up for the morning.

Chapter Fourteen

When Emily's leg was finally healed, she began to bring the child again to Laura's house. She also had difficulty in dealing with Mauro. Once again, she became annoyed again to Laura's lover. But in those moments, she decided not to be complacent with him. She assured herself that Mauro would not make a way to get close to her.

Emily knew that Mauro had done a great thing for her safety. But she had to distance herself for the peace of all. She also knew what kind of person Laura was.

She knew Laura's blood was boiling on her, but she could just calm herself if it were for Michael. However, she insisted not to create a mess so that the two wouldn't meet at the point of anger.

But the opportunity to speak to each other was still unavoidable.

When Emily and Mauro met in the kitchen, Mauro tried to avoid Emily, but he couldn't do it.

"How are you?" asked Mauro to the lady.

"I'm fine," Emily said with hesitance.

"Next time, you must be careful, especially in the crowded area."

Emily just nodded and left the place where they were. However, Mauro soon followed Emily. At that time, Laura was about to enter the room that Mauro didn't expect.

"Why are you still here, and you're not leaving my condo yet?" Laura asked Emily.

"I'm leaving. I've just returned something to the kitchen," Emily defended herself.

"Why? Do you want to flirt with my boyfriend Mauro first?"

"I don't understand what you're saying!" Emily suddenly turned her back to Laura.

"Don't just turn away when I'm talking to you!" Laura snapped at Emily.

"What is your problem?"

"You flirt with my boyfriend!"

"I don't know what you're talking about!"

"Leave my boyfriend alone!"

"You know, you are beautiful, but you're full of self-insecurities! I don't care about your boyfriend!"

Emily left after saying that.

"You don't want to stop, ah!" threatened Laura.

In those moments, Laura was still dissatisfied with how she dealt with Emily. One day, Laura meant to seduce Luigi. Luigi was shocked, but he was sure that Laura just wanted to piss Emily. Laura did her plan at the time that Emily was about to come home.

Emily saw how Laura leaned over Luigi's neck. Emily didn't like it, but she didn't fall to the role-play of Luigi's ex-wife, Laura.

"You have a visitor!" Emily's words were jealous, but she tried to act normal.

"Oh! Your helper is here," Laura teased. Emily didn't feel wrong about Laura's words.

"She is not my helper. She is my fiancé, and we're about to get married. Remember, our marriage is over, as stated in the annulment, and you're not in place for insulting my fiancé!" Luigi told Laura.

"You're just going to replace me, and then you've got a helper! What does she know? Washing your butt or cleaning the house?"

"That's enough! You're not in your house to insult Emily!"

Emily just looked at her. Knowing what her status was in life, she wouldn't be intimidated by Laura.

"I feel sorry for you. No one cares about you in your world, so here you are seeking our attention!" said Emily.

"I'm a diamond that shines, so everyone dazzles when they see me glowing. And you, what are you? A rag that can be put in the trash anytime when not needed anymore!"

"A rag, even it is rubbish, it cannot be simply disposed of.

It can be washed, and after that, it will be placed in the cabinet and will be retaken in time of need!"

"It's still rubbish! It'll be used again and again, and still, it will be thrown away. Unlike a diamond, it needs to be kept and put in the bank deposit box for safekeeping. But to you, anytime, it can be thrown away."

"There are jewels that need to be kept and stored in banks' deposit boxes if needed. But if you wear them, they can be dropped off like glittering earrings, bracelets or necklaces. In the time that they are gone, they don't have value anymore. Like you, when your ex-husband lost his love for you, where are you now?"

"You don't have any glitter to him either. I am the diamond that shines in his eyes and is hidden in his heart. And not you!" Laura finally stopped from Emily's utterings, something she hadn't expected from Emily's mouth.

In those moments, Luigi came in between the arguing of the two.

"Your nanny is a rascal, has no respect!" said Laura.

"You're the one who started it," Luigi said.

Luigi pulled Laura out of his condo unit. Laura had done nothing with what Luigi did until she finally got out of the condo.

In the parking area where her car was parked, Mauro was there waiting for her inside the car. Laura angrily opened the car door. And as she sat down, she pulled the car door toward her, something that Mauro wondered.

"I told you not to go here anymore because I know it will just ruin your day," Mauro said.

"That girl is annoying! I will not stop her until she is out of my son's path!"

"Just make sure your son is the problem, and you have no plans to return to your ex-husband!"

The two looked at each other, but Laura suddenly turned her glance away from Mauro.

She then looked at her vast surroundings. Until they reached home, Laura was still silent.

She just kept pounding, which Mauro couldn't stop. As a result, they fought more.

As the door opened, she quickly removed and threw the bag over the sofa. This warmed Mauro's head further.

"What exactly is your problem? Why are you so mean?" asked Mauro.

"Nothing!"

"Your mouth is almost like a volcano. Your anger is out of control!"

"Nothing, I said!"

She threw the vase that was placed over the edge of the cabinet. Mauro was surprised at Laura's behavior in front of him.

Mauro also acted quickly and took the vase that rested on top of the center table. He also threw it in front of Laura.

Mauro was still not satisfied, and he approached Laura. She quickly grabbed Laura's face with both hands, something the woman had not expected.

"Do not act like that in front of me when you are hot-tempered! You are just famous, but your personality is rotten. Do you know that you are tiring to see because of your behavior?!" Mauro said angrily. "Are you going away? Let's see who will lose so much! "

"Don't scare me! I can take you back to the place where you left!" said Laura.

Laura was shocked at Mauro's behavior. She noticed that he was fighting against her.

She thought she might lose her job by the time she appeared in the Press People, and Mauro might have made a lousy story against her.

But she still managed to be calm, then went inside the bedroom.

Laura's anger was restrained to Mauro's behavior. She didn't expect that she would find out about her boyfriend's behavior.

She made sure the door was locked so that Mauro couldn't open.

Until the darkness reached her, Laura still did not go out of her room. In the living room, Mauro's actions were just normal, as if nothing happened. He didn't worry about Laura for not coming out of her room. Mauro just thought that she still loved him and had no plans to divorce him. But Mauro didn't realize that Laura was planning to drive out from the condo.

"Where are you going?" Mauro asked Laura. He noticed that she was carrying a small suitcase containing her personal belongings.

"Let's finish this!" Laura said firmly to her lover.

"You can't do this to me!"

"I'm sorry. I've made my decision. I still love Luigi, that's why I am acting like this!" Suddenly tears came to her eyes.

"Sorry about what happened a while ago. I was just shocked. It will not happen again!" Mauro pleaded to her.

"I have decided. I'm sorry. I can't live without my son and my husband. I love my family!"

"No, no!"

In those moments, Emily was coming. She was nearing the gate. She had decided to return the key because there would be a new nanny who will bring Michael during his schedule to Laura.

Emily was in the hallway when she heard a strange noise from Laura's condo. She quickly opened the door, since she has her key, to see what was going on inside.

Emily panicked. She saw Laura bloody lying on the floor. Emily also saw a hard vase that was next to Laura's head. She quickly grabbed it and made sure that it was the reason for the accident.

When Mauro arrived from outside, Emily looked up.

"What did you do to her?!" Mauro said sternly to Emily.

"I just caught Señora lying on the floor!"

"I'll call the police!"

"No, I didn't do it!"

A few minutes later, the police arrived. Emily's two hands were quickly handcuffed. She just cried because of her self-pity until they went out of the condo. Mauro followed them as well.

Emily's face was filled with sadness. It was like beyond the fall of heaven and earth. Upon arriving inside the police station, Emily was grabbed by a mugshot and fingerprint. She never expected this to happen to her.

When Luigi arrived with Michael, Emily's consciousness went back to where she thought her friends had come.

"Why did you do all that to mommy?!" the boy told her right.

"I don't know what you're talking about. I don't know about the killing of your mommy!"

"You killed my mommy! You killed my mommy!"

Suddenly the boy walked away and approached his father. Luigi felt pity for her.

"Why did you do that?!" Luigi told Emily.

"I'm not the one who killed Laura!"

"How are you? How are we, and how can you convince me that you didn't do it then? You and Laura are always fighting!"

"Laura and I indeed have a dispute, but that doesn't mean I'll be able to kill her!"

"Is that because of Mauro, who's obsessed with you?!"

Emily was shocked when Luigi told her.

"Do you even believe them that I'm getting her boyfriend?"

"Is it true?!"

Emily didn't answer Luigi's accusation against her. She just turned away and ignored his words.

When she tried to approach Michael to kiss him, he turned away. She could do nothing but cry over what had happened to her. And she had been brought into the cell.

"Why did you do that to your tata?" said his father.

"She's bad at what she did to Mommy!" said Michael.

"We are not yet sure about that. Maybe your tata was just falsely accused!"

"Why Mauro said that to the court?" huffed Michael.

"We will find out by the time she will be brought to trial!"

The child does not care yet in such words. All he knew in those moments was that even though he loved her tata, she still did something terrible to his mommy.

During those moments, Luigi noticed that at Michael's seven years of age, he saw the emotion he had for his parent. And he thought that it was Emily who had killed his mother, Laura.

Luigi was impressed by his son's decision to move away from his tata Emily first even though he knew for himself that it would be difficult. Because in any angle, he lost his mommy. The child believed that his tata committed the crime. So, the father could do nothing to force him to come and visit his tata, who was imprisoned.

"No more, Daddy. I'll just play with Minerva!"

Although Luigi was shocked at his child's response, he noticed that the world of the child was turned upside down.

He used to look for his tata right away.

Luigi wondered that Michael refused to go with him so that they can visit his tata. He couldn't force him because the boy's anger prevailed over his father's girlfriend.

Luigi was with the lawyer for Emily to solve his girlfriend's problem. He looked at his girlfriend, Emily. Luigi pitied her. He never imagined that his girlfriend could end the life of his ex-wife, Laura. His mind was arguing. For the last few days, Emily and Laura were in conflict. He did not expect that it would now end like this. Luigi couldn't help but be trapped in this situation. Who between them was more deserving of giving importance — Emily or his ex-wife Laura in defending her right to justice?

Chapter Fifteen

In Luigi and Michael's mansion, they returned since Laura's death. They stayed at the palace even though it was too big for only two people and housekeepers.

During Michael's silence, Minerva was shocked at what the boy had told her.

"What?!" Minerva panicked.

"I said, let's get my toys at Mommy's condo," Michael said.

"But we can't go there, and it's scary!"

"If you don't come with me, I'll go alone. I'll just go with our driver, Ambo."

Minerva was hit by her conscience. She was forced to go with the boy's wishes even though she was afraid of her former boss Laura who died in the condo.

"Alright! I'll go with you!"

After a while, they quickly left with their driver, Ambo.

They were already in Laura's condo. Minerva's face was filled with fear and awe, but Michael had no trace of fear. He noticed that his legs were pulled further into the condo. But he didn't mind that because what was important to him at those times was to get what he wanted to get in his mother's condo.

He took all his toys one by one. The boy's actions were casual, but Minerva nearly rolled her eyes, looking at the surroundings. She thought ghosts were real, and that her former boss, Laura, might show to her.

They were about to leave the room when Laura's phone suddenly rang. The boy did not expect it, and this led him to wonder. He would have ignored it and have continued to go out, but it seemed like something made to drag his feet. Minerva just followed Michael. It took a long time before Michael saw the phone. He needed more attention to know where that sound came from until Michael found it inside the cabinet. Michael quickly opened it and picked up the phone, but it died suddenly.

However, he just took it and went out of the room of his mother.

Inside the car, Michael looked at his mother's phone again. He input the password since he had memorized it every time, he used it when playing games. Michael was surprised when he looked at the call history and noticed that no number had come out of the call during the hours they had been in Laura's room. At such a young age, he didn't even think about what it meant. All he did was open the games he always used to play.

He still remembered that he was always confined to his room for his mother's phone.

They often argued because of this, but the mother had nothing to do with her child's behavior until Michael would fell asleep as he played. As usual, the boy quickly fell asleep as he played until Ambo picked him up and put him inside his room. Minerva placed

Michael's toys, and even the phone he tried to open, on the bed beside him.

In the child's room, he was unaware that his mother's phone was ringing again, but he just ignored it. The sound was gone for the meantime, but it rang again, which surprised Michael. His eyes widened before he finally scanned his mother's phone. But he was surprised to find that he didn't even find a number on his screen.

The child was already frightened by the incident. He thought his mother was scaring him and was making Michael feel Laura, something that had just happened to him.

"Mommy? Is that you?"

The child could feel the fear, but he needed to know what those sounds mean. At his young age, that was what puzzled on his mind.

"Do you need my help?" Tears wanted to flow down Michael's cheeks. "Mommy, who did this to you? Was it tata?!" Michael said angrily. "Was it Tata Emily?!" he repeated it. Michael was looking for a place to go so that he can tell his mother that he loved her even though he was naughty and mean to his mother.

His mother's phone rang again. He grabbed it, and its screen suddenly opened. There, he scanned the screen. When it suddenly opened, Michael watched the video inside.

He was shocked, and his eyes widened at what he had witnessed. What he watched surprised him.

"No!"

Michael burst into tears due to what he witnessed. He couldn't believe what he saw.

"Mommy, mommy!"

From the housemates' room, Minerva was startled by the child's constant crying and forced her to go to Michael's room.

"Why are you still awake? And what are you weeping for? " asked Minerva.

"Mommy, my poor Mommy!" said Michael to Minerva.

When she looked at the phone and looked at its screen, she saw nothing. Minerva was horrified to what Michael said. She looked deeply and couldn't believe what the child was saying.

Inside the cell, Emily had no enthusiasm when Luigi visited. She thought his beloved had just been forced to visit her because of what happened to his ex-wife, Laura. She still faced him even though she felt her feet were heavy to get near to Luigi.

"If you're tired of coming here because you think I did that to your ex-wife, then it's best for you not to come back."

"Because both of you have always been quarrelling, even in front of me. That's why I can't help but think that you will do it!"

"It just means you doubt me that I did something to your wife!"

"Is it true that it was you?!"

"If you don't trust me, you can leave!"

"Emily, wait!"

Emily turned away. She never answered Luigi's accusations against her. He was puzzled about Emily, who might then be angry at him.

Luigi left, but the two did not have a clear argument.

Mauro, meanwhile, gave all the pieces of evidence he had. This would vehemently accuse Emily of killing Laura, something she couldn't accept.

Emily was confused about what happened to her. She didn't know what to do. She couldn't even trust Luigi, too, because he had many questions that left him confused about the crime. Luigi suspected Emily of hitting Laura with a jar vase on the head. Emily was confused. She had been involved twice with troubles she never wanted.

The child she loved and cared for until he was seven years old was already aloof to her. The child was so determined not even to visit her. Emily thought it was Luigi who told Michael not to visit her. She felt sorry for herself.

The next day, Emily had another hearing. In that case, if there would be no evidence to prove her innocence, she would be incarcerated. Her only prayer was for her mother and father, not to know what had happened to her. It was because she couldn't forgive herself when something would happen to her.

But she had prepared herself for the consequences of her case.

She felt sorry for herself when she drove Luigi away and did not talk to him properly. She didn't know if she had made the right decision for herself to do all those things.

"How's Michael doing, uh?" That was all she said, and she continued to cry.

On the other hand, she would still prepare herself because she had no fault with what happened to Laura. That's what Emily had in mind. In those moments, she was holding a rosary. She faithfully used the bead of every misery of Christ until she had completed it.

Inside the court, Emily's feet were heavy as she was walking toward the court hearing. She did not leave her rosary she bought inside the Vatican. All she wanted was to have freedom of mind and to have the truth that would cross in her case. She was seated at a long table with her lawyer. It was inevitable that her heart would growl as her boyfriend, Luigi would take the witness stand.

"I didn't know it would go this way. I told her to go to Laura's condo and apologize. But I didn't know that this would lead to everything," Luigi said before the court. Emily just looked at him because Luigi told the right thing. She would also return the key to Laura then.

"I saw Emily holding the jar vase that she used to hit Laura's head!" said Mauro.

In those moments, Emily just shook her head over what Mauro had said before the court.

A voice broke the silence of the court. Suddenly Michael came. Even this boy made a loud noise in the court that made Luigi and the people in the courtroom surprised. One of the persons who was surprised was the Judge who would examine Emily's case.

The Judge criticized Michael and prevented the child from driving him out of the court. He spoke to him while Michael was sitting at the Judge's desk.

"Why did you come into the court so suddenly? Are you looking for something here?" asked the Judge.

"It's because of tata Emily," the boy said.

"Why? What do you know about Emily? "

Everyone on the panel was shocked, especially his father. That surprised Emily, too. But in those moments, Mauro carefully watched what Michael had to say in court.

"It's not Emily who killed my mom, Laura Papi!" Michael said it out loud in court.

Everyone was startled by what they heard from the boy. However, the Judge was keen to learn the truth from the boy who surprised him.

"Why do you say that your tata Emily did not commit the act of murdering your mother? Were you there? Did you see who did that to your mom?"

"I didn't see it, but I saw it in the video!"

It was at that moment that Emily looked at the boy. She felt a sense of fright from the words he would convey.

"Are you holding the video, so that we can show it in front of the court?"

At that moment, the child was already sitting in front of the witness stand to explain. His father, Luigi, was more scared because he didn't expect his son to come to court. Even though the father was concerned, he just trusted his son.

In those moments, Michael quickly reached for the phone containing a video confirming that his tata Emily was not responsible for his mother's death. Hon. Judge Ricardo Casilino already had the video containing a mysterious man who took over the life of Michael's mother. He tried to open the video several times but had found nothing to prove that Emily did not murder Michael's mother.

"Empty!" said the Judge.

Michael quickly took it to Hon. Ricardo Casilino to make sure that the video was there. He was even shocked by what he witnessed. Later on, his father saw that his son, Michael, was depressed.

At that moment, everyone in the courtroom was stunned. Suddenly, Michael stood at the witness stand. But everything came to an abrupt halt as the projector opened, and the light hit the wall. The video content was shown there. Everyone was amazed at what they saw. A man took over Laura's life.

Mauro saw it. He was the one in the video. It was apparent how Mauro had slammed the jar vase to Laura inside her condo. They also saw how shocked he was when Emily suddenly went there. Mauro took advantage of Emily's entry into the room. At the window with the fire exit, he went out of the condo.

The video showed where Emily entered, was also where Mauro came in and pretended to have witnessed the incident himself.

At that moment, Mauro quickly got up to run away. But Michael's eyes were quick, and he promptly pointed out that Mauro was about to flee. Luigi was then ready, so he quickly attacked Mauro, and the two were already fighting.

"You're the one who killed my ex-wife! Now, you will end up in jail!"

Emily wept in those moments. She felt like a massive thorn was removed in her chest.

A miracle was like told, and everyone was shocked while nobody moved the projector to see the truth. This served as a way to find out what happened to Laura. Even Judge Hon. Ricardo Casilino couldn't believe it. But the fact was shown that Emily was innocent, Michael's tata.

It was at that moment that Luigi approached Emily quickly.

"Sorry!"

Emily nodded with tears in her eyes, and Luigi hugged her.

"Sorry, tata!" said Michael.

Emily wept, and she quickly embraced the boy who had brought the good news.

"I should be the one to thank you!" said Emily.

"No, it was Mommy who gave me the information. In my dream, she said I would help her," said Michael, which surprised the two. "Mommy is in the courtroom!"

Luigi suddenly spoke in the air.

"Thank you, Laura. Trust us that we will never leave our son, Michael, alone."

Laura was just around the corner and had a good smile when she heard those words from her ex-husband that he and Emily would not leave their son,

Michael. It was during those moments that Emily also repeated those words to Laura in air.

Sunday at Via Urbana in Sta. Prudinziana, they all went to church. After that, Emily was surprised at what Luigi had done to her. He knelt before her and before the crowd. A small box was taken, and it contained a ring.

"Will you marry me?!" Luigi said as he knelt in front of Emily.

He offered the ring as a token of his loyal love.

"Yes!"

THE END.

About the Author

When I was 15 years old, my mother noticed that I can write. So, I continued my writing. Which is one of the Publications in the Philippines it is GASI, or Graphic Art Service incorporation. Until I got used to it, a few more years of learning, even writing like articles, in showbiz has also been done. One of the things that gave me to write an article again was when covid-19 started, and also, I will write an article Filipino Community based in Rome Italy by Lisa Bueno since 2008 until 2012, then Akit Magazine to give way to continue my passion. Started again. Until 2018, I have continued writing until now. Of the (7) seven siblings, I am the third eldest.

- Philippines History Education/Rome Italy.
- Bulacan Standard Academy graduated High school 1980.
- Manila (Pandacan Manila) SCRIPTWRITING 1982
- Roma, Italy Danielle Manin High school graduated 2013
- Scuole International Di Comics (associate of arts narrative base 2015
- Alison Empowered (Ireland) Business Communication skills 2023